The Secret Diary of Ashley Juergens

The Secret Diary of Ashley Juergens

ASHLEY JUERGENS

HYPERION

New York

Library of Congress Cataloging-in-Publication Data

The secret diary of Ashley Juergens / Ashley Juergens.
p. cm.
Fictitiously attributed to Ashley Juergens, a character on the ABC television
show, The secret life of the American teenager.
ISBN 978-1-4013-2407-0
1. Teenagers—United States—Fiction. I. Secret life of the American
teenager (Television program)
PS3600.A1S43 2010
813'.6—dc22   2010008966

Hyperion books are available for special promotions and premiums. For details
contact the HarperCollins Special Markets Department in the New York office
at 212-207-7528, fax 212-207-7222, or e-mail spsales@harpercollins.com.

Book design by Chris Welch

FIRST EDITION

10 9 8 7 6 5 4 3 2 1

THIS LABEL APPLIES TO TEXT STOCK

The Secret Diary of Ashley Juergens

Sept. 1st

Today I was sent to the principal's office because Mrs. Sallinger claimed I flashed her when I raised my hand to tell her exactly when Custer's Last Stand was. According to her, my shirt was so short my belly button was showing and it was distracting to her and the other students. Like they were even awake. I can't believe she punished the only person actually following her lesson plan. She didn't even let me answer the question, and if anyone cares, it was 1876. Isn't whether or not I'm paying attention in class more important than what I'm wearing? Yes, I did really ask Mrs. Sallinger this question and I made it clear it was not meant to be

1

rhetorical. It was at that moment my teacher used what little power she had to send me, Ashley Juergens, to the principal's office.

I had to sit out in the hall next to a cheater, a class clown who got everyone to do the wave whenever his teacher turned to write on the board, and someone who had carved his name into his locker. And I was being reprimanded because my choice of clothes that day had been a poor one, or at least that's what Principal Miller told me. Actually, she said my choice of clothes is always poor. It was poor last year and I'm continuing to make poor fashion choices this year. At least I'm consistent, because that's one thing a lot of kids aren't these days. She said she and the other teachers have been watching me. Apparently I'm on their "list." Wow. They have a piece of paper in their possession with my name written on it. I'm really shaking now.

Principal Miller could see her attempts to frighten me into submission were not working so she went on to Phase Two of the school authority playbook: shame.

That didn't work because I am not ashamed of my stomach or my belly button or any other part of my body. That's why I wear clothes that show them off. If anything, she should be ashamed of the way she runs this school. I told Principal Miller if I ran the school I would add sex education to the curriculum, I would pass out free condoms to whichever students wanted them and even the ones who didn't, and I would make *Spring Awakening* this year's fall production. I think the parents would really enjoy it.

She told me she would take my suggestions into consideration. Yeah right. I could tell she was getting desperate because she started using words my parents always use when they lecture me. And since I'm missing my grammar test while she goes on and on and on, I will give you the words and how she used them in a sentence: **Appropriate**: "This is an institution of learning, Ashley, and it is just not *appropriate* for you to be learning with your legs and stomach so exposed." **Young lady**: "You are thirteen years old and as a *young lady* it is important to carry yourself as such by wearing the correct attire." **Proper**: "It is just not *proper* to wear a skirt that is so short and leaves so little to the imagination." **Image**: "The *image* you are presenting to your peers is of someone who is more interested in showing off her physical assets than her mental ones."

So unoriginal, right? And now, my rebuttal:

If this is an institution of learning, then why did you feel it was *appropriate* to drag me out of class to talk about something that has absolutely nothing to do with the learning process? And as a *young lady* who is old enough to make up her own mind, I feel it is only *proper* to leave my wardrobe decisions up to me. As for the *image* I present to my peers, it is of someone who is confident with her mind and body, which is why I was raising my hand to answer Mrs. Sallinger's question, unconcerned with how I looked at the time.

I think the real reason I got into trouble was because I expressed my individuality. It tends to scare authority figures when someone my age does that. It's a conspiracy, really. Think about it. At school I, as a student, am forced to follow the same schedule every day. I must respond to the call of bells that tell me where to go and when to eat and I have to raise my hand to ask and answer questions. It's like some weird, constant Pavlovian experiment. I am sent to the principal's office because I refuse to be conditioned. I told Principal Miller my theory and she said I was paranoid.

I made sure to get in a few eye rolls and heavy sighs to let Principal Miller know I wasn't taking this conversation too seriously. She threw the attitude card at me, which I continued to hold up the entire time we talked. I thought I made some good points but she was too busy staring at my belly button to notice. She continued lecturing me by raising her voice like she was playing to the cheap seats even though we were the only people in the room and were sitting just a few feet apart. I could hear the cheater, class clown, and locker tagger snicker from out in the hallway. I wasn't crazy about them being privy to our conversation but we were all in the same boat—I had to listen to the dumb reasons they were there when I was stuck waiting out in the hallway.

Then Principal Miller started fishing through the dreaded lost-and-found box. I told her I hadn't lost anything I wanted found. She said that's okay and then took out one of our ugly school sweatshirts. I told her I wasn't cold but thanks for her concern. She said my belly button looked cold so she was giving me this sweatshirt to wear for the rest of the day. On second thought, she added, since it hadn't been claimed for two weeks, it was mine to keep. I said I couldn't take something that didn't belong to me and then she said she insisted, which meant I either put on the sweatshirt or got detention, and as much as I dread going home, especially after my parents find out I was sent to the principal's office, I hate detention more. They stick you in a room with all the creative and enlightened students and force you not to talk to each other. I know what you're thinking, the locker tagger is enlightened? Well, for your information, we had a lovely conversation out in the hall where he explained that scratching his name into his locker was not a simple and uncouth act of rebellion, but rather a social commentary on what ownership really means in today's public school system. He also thought my Pavlovian School Theory had some real validity.

Principal Miller made me put on my Scarlet sweatshirt as she continued talking about other ways I could respect the school community through my sartorial choices: pants (preferably long and baggy), skirts (length preferably below the knee), long-sleeve shirts (preferably to the wrist), sweatshirts (preferably the one she just gave me), hats, scarves, gloves, socks (preferably knee length), turtlenecks, coats, jackets (preferably big and bulky), sweaters (preferably long and loose), and, when in doubt, layer, layer, layer!

Too bad I like to peel, peel, peel!

After listening to her you would think winter was twelve months out of the year. That or I should join a sorority for the perpetually cold.

I told her if I'm being forced to dress like I'm in Catholic school, then the least she could do is wear a habit. She didn't go for it. Needless to say, I don't have any of those things hanging in my closet. I could probably borrow a scarf from Amy to keep in my locker in case of emergencies, which brings us to Phase Three of Principal Miller's lecture: Why can't you be more like your sister, Amy?

Amy is fifteen and we are nothing alike. I'm opinionated, I'm sarcastic, I'm funny, and I will tell you what I really think even if it's going to hurt your feelings because brutally honest is the best way to be. I like to wear short skirts and tight shirts while Amy wears long, loose tops and has never met a scarf she didn't like. I wish everyone would stop telling me to be more like Amy and support my decision to be me. I'm not so bad if they would just give me a chance and not take everything I say and wear so personally.

I thought since Amy had moved on to high school the powers that be would leave me alone, but I'm still being compared to little Miss Goody Two-shoes. I'm sure Principal Miller really misses her. Amy never got into trouble. I don't think she ever stepped foot inside this office. Amy actually got an award for perfect attendance. That means she didn't take one sick day, even when she was sick. How am I supposed to compete with someone who shows up to school even when her immune system's down? Plus, Amy always got good grades and did exactly as she was told. It was mortifying. They probably never had a file on her like mine, which Principal Miller is probably currently writing in. With a red pen.

Amy was never forced to wear a school sweatshirt that was two sizes too big and smelled like someone's gym shoes. It looked hideous, but Principal Miller thought it looked great. It made me think I should have my own billboard like those anti-fur ads. But instead of saying, "I'd rather go naked than wear fur," mine would say, "I'd rather go naked than follow this school's dress code." I wonder how much it costs to rent that billboard across the street. . . .

Principal Miller said she knows I dress the way I do for attention and if I wanted to express myself I should find another way to do it. Then I walked right into her trap and asked in what other way was I supposed to express myself? She searched in her desk and handed me a notebook. This notebook. I thought she was going to make me take notes as she went over the school dress code for the hundredth time but instead she told me keeping a journal is an excellent way to express oneself.

I just stared at her. I guess she couldn't tell I was being sarcastic when I asked for another way to express myself, because I am very good at doing just that. I am extremely vocal about my thoughts and opinions. That is why I think journals are stupid. Because if you can't say what you are feeling out loud, then what good does writing those feelings down in a book and then shoving it in your desk do? And those are the exact words I said to Principal Miller. She didn't really answer me. She said I have to write in this stupid thing and turn it in at the end of each month so she can review how my

Principal Miller actually called it a diary, but diaries are for girls ten years old and younger who write "Property Of" and their names on the outside while keeping it closed with a heart-shaped lock in order to hide the boring details of their lives no one wants to read anyway. So since I'm being forced to write one myself, I'm calling it a journal. Property of Ashley Juergens. Read at your own risk.

new creative outlet is coming along. So I'm forced to fill up these pages with something or suffer the consequences. I wonder if she hands a notebook out to every student who's called in here. I bet there are stacks of these in her closet she's never even read. Oh well, on to the journaling . . . (and yes, I'm being sarcastic here, too).

I wanted to make sure my sweatshirt got back to the lost-and-found box safe and sound so as soon as I made it out of the principal's office I went into the girls' bathroom and left it hanging in one of the stalls. I know you will find a way to get this sweatshirt back to me, Principal Miller, but until then I would rather not smell like someone's gym shoes. I think that would be more distracting to my teachers and fellow students than my deeply scandalous belly button.

Principal Miller also took the liberty of calling my dad and letting him know about my indiscretion. I could hear my dad's side of the phone call from the hallway: "Ashley did what? . . . Belly button? . . . No, I agree, it's completely inappropriate and her mother and I will have a talk with her about this. . . . You are absolutely right, she is a *young lady* and needs to dress like one. . . . No, this is not the *proper image* our daughter should be putting out there and we will make sure she wears more *appropriate* clothes from now on."

See, there are those lecture words again. I hope next time we meet, Principal Miller, you have come up with some new ones. Let's at least try to mix things up a little bit. I also have plenty of other conspiracy theories I would like to share with you. They involve the Pep Squad and the school's drinking fountains.

Dad was still on the phone with Principal Miller when I heard him move on to Phase Three: "I agree, she could learn a thing or two from her sister. . . . I'm sorry, what did you say? . . . Sex education? . . . Condoms? . . . *Spring Awakening?*"

I'm in trouble now.

Wait until my mom finds out about this. The last time this happened she made me put on a "modest fashion show" so she could approve my school outfits ahead of time. Ugh, I can hear the lecture already: I'll walk back and forth in front of her modeling the latest Amish trends while she tells me how a cardigan buttoned up to my chin really brings out my eyes. That's when I'll tell her an unbuttoned cardigan really brings out my boobs. Being rebellious is so much work with all the talking and the listening you have to do.

Dad's lecture was pretty standard: it involved telling me I'm not sexy and shouldn't dress that way because I'm not ready to have sex. I actually agree with my dad, not that I told him that. I'm not ready to have sex, so I'm not having sex. But just because I'm dressing the way I dress doesn't mean

I'm sending out some kind of bat signal to all the boys that I'm ready to have sex with them. I just want to dress how I want to dress. I'm thirteen! Next year, like Amy, I will be in high school.

7:30 P.M.

I passed Amy in the hallway on the way to the dining room and she looked like she had seen a ghost. She had such a death grip on the handle of her French horn case that I said she must be hiding something really important in there. She freaked out and asked me why I would think that. Geez, she can't even take a joke. I was going to ask how her first day of high school was but she went straight into the bathroom. She even took her French horn in with her. I know she really loves playing that thing, but that was ridiculous. Isn't there anybody in this house I can have a decent conversation with?

Dad asked how Principal Miller punished me at school. I told him going to school was my punishment.

I have to figure out where I'm going to hide this thing. It has to be somewhere my parents and Amy never look. . . . I've got it. I'll hide it in my duvet. But if my dad does happen to find it, I'd just like to say: Dad, I'm not having sex, I've never had sex, and I'm not planning to have sex for a while.

During dinner, Amy sided with my dad after he lectured me again about my clothes. He said he was going to keep it

up until I changed out of the of-
fending outfit. Sorry, Dad. Not going to happen.

No way am I telling my dad about this journal. He'll think I'm using it as some sordid diary to document all the sex I'm having.

And thanks, Amy, for backing up
your sister, as usual.

Amy's been moody ever since she got back from band
camp. You'd think this would bring us closer because I'm
usually pretty moody but it hasn't. Amy hardly speaks and
when she does, it's only "yes" or "no" answers. I tried acting
interested and asked about band camp but she didn't want to
talk about it. She said she played her French horn and
marched around and that's all there is to know. That's pretty
much what I thought happened. I don't get why you have to
go to band camp to practice the same things you already
practice at school but it's Mom and Dad's money.

The other day I Googled "geekiest band instrument" and
here's what came up: (1.) French Horn, (2.) Tuba, (3.) Clari-
net, (4.) French Horn, (5.) Cymbals. That's right, Google con-
siders the French horn so nerdy it listed it twice. I told Amy
she should have gone with the saxophone, but she never takes
my advice.

Amy being at band camp made this past summer the BEST
SUMMER EVER (or so I'd say if I was prone to that sort of
hyperbole). I had the house all to myself and pretended I was
an only child. I didn't have to listen to Amy play her French
horn all the time and I didn't have to see her two annoying
best friends, Lauren and Madison. Lauren is such a snob and
Madison is the worst gossip ever. Dad was pretty busy at the

furniture store and working really late hours so he wasn't really around either. My mom pretty much left me alone to watch my *Twilight Zone* and movie marathons. She still complained about my clothes, which were not *appropriate* even though it was summer and this *young lady* was hot.

It was quiet with Amy not around. I didn't hear from her while she was away except for one night when she called my cell phone. She sounded funny, like she was upset or something, almost like she'd been crying, but she told me she was just tired. I asked if she wanted to talk to Mom or Dad. She said no, she wanted to talk to me. I waited for her to say something but she said never mind. She was just homesick and wanted to hear my voice. When she got home I asked her what had happened that night to make her want to call me, but she acted like she didn't know what I was talking about. She hasn't said much else to me since.

8:32 P.M.

Amy's mood lifted a little bit after dinner. Some guy called her. If you know Amy at all you would think I was lying because she has never, ever had a boy call her at home. Well, there was that one time in seventh grade, but they were doing a science project together and he had to call her. But this was the first time a boy called of his own free will just to talk to her. And he was nervous, too. I know because I was the one who answered the phone. I wouldn't have believed he was calling for Amy if I hadn't heard it for myself. His voice was very squeaky and he spoke like he was reading what he wanted to say off of a piece of paper when he asked me, "Is Amy Juergens home and could I please speak with her if she isn't busy?" When I asked him to identify himself he told me his name was Ben Boykewich. I told him I'd never heard Amy mention his name before. This seemed to catch him off guard because he started stammering but eventually was able to explain they had spoken in the hallway at school today and he was calling to ask her something. I told Amy a boy was calling her and she looked as surprised as I was. Mom and Dad couldn't believe it either, but were very excited a boy was interested in Amy. Well, Mom was. Dad was more cautiously excited/concerned.

Amy and Ben's conversation was pretty short, but from what I could hear Amy didn't remember the hallway conversation this Ben guy thought was so memorable. But she agreed to go out with him anyway. At least it made Mom and Dad forget about me getting in trouble at school, which was a nice side effect. This guy Ben isn't so bad. Amy and Ben are going to the high school football game and then to some dance. This is Amy's first date. I was happy for her until my parents told me I have to go to the football game with them so we can watch Amy march around the field with the rest of the band. They even suggested I go to the dance. They want me to dress like a little Victorian doll but also go to a dance with my sister and all two of her high school friends? No wonder teenagers are so confused.

The dance is being put together by Grace Bowman's church. She goes to school with Amy. And to make everything worse (because that's what Mom and Dad love to do) my parents have final approval over my outfit before I walk out the door to a place I don't even want to go. I was able to talk them out of chaperoning in exchange for wearing a turtleneck.

Sept. 2nd

6:30 P.M.

That guy Ben just came to pick up Amy. His voice was still squeaky. It was kind of annoying but Amy seemed to think it was cute. The way Mom and Dad were acting you would think Amy and Ben were going to the prom or something. They were all over Ben, telling him when Amy's curfew is and to call if they were going to be late. Dad even yelled after them not to have sex as they were walking down the driveway and the look on Amy's and Ben's faces was great. When they aren't embarrassing me, it is really fun to watch Mom and Dad embarrass Amy.

Ben's dad was sitting in the car with the engine running so my dad ran out and introduced himself, but it turned out to be Ben's driver. My dad seemed relieved there was some sort of chaperone, even if it was a driver. This guy Ben must have a lot of money, or he spent everything he had just to impress Amy.

9:35 P.M.

Mom and Dad and I just got back from the game. It was not exciting. It alternated between guys running into each other and my sister marching around in place with the rest of the band. She's gotten better at marching—she only ran into someone once—so maybe band camp was worth it after all. I hope high school is more exciting by the time I get there.

My dad kept talking over the band to remind me that guys like nice girls and that's why that Ben guy called Amy. He was talking so loud people were starting to stare, so I kept my eyes on the field. That's when I noticed this majorette named Adrian surrounded by a ton of guys, and I don't think my dad would label her "nice." Her uniform was a lot shorter than the other majorettes'. That outfit would get her sent to your office for sure, Principal Miller. And she would definitely receive a complimentary sweatshirt. I didn't bring any of this up to my dad because I didn't want to start debating his bogus theory in public.

Then I spotted a lot of guys staring at Grace, one of the cheerleaders, and she's a nice girl, so maybe Dad and I are both wrong. I noticed Amy kept staring at the drummer in the band, I think his name is Ricky, and Ricky kept staring at Adrian. I remember seeing Ricky when we dropped Amy off at band camp. Amy was pretty excited when she saw him there, too. I guess they didn't hit it off because she's the only girl out there he isn't paying attention to.

I felt bad for Amy until I looked over and saw Ben watching the game with his two friends, Henry and Alice. Ben never took his eyes off Amy during the whole game. I wonder if Amy is going out with Ben to try to get Ricky's attention. If that's the case, it's not working. I hope she gives Ben a chance because he really likes her. Sure, his voice is squeaky and he has a lot of nervous energy and he doesn't have much musical talent, but maybe he can get her out of this funk she's been in lately.

Sept. 5th

3:17 P.M.

I've changed my mind about the whole "journals are stupid" thing.

After coming home from school and being reminded how crazy my family is, this notebook will be very handy in documenting my story if I ever decide to make good on my threat to divorce my parents and seek emancipation. I know what you're thinking, that I'm all snark and no action. Well, you're wrong.

When I was eight years old I got into a big fight with my parents because they insisted I take up the recorder, since Amy had so much fun playing the French horn. I argued that being able to play "Hot Cross Buns" (also known as "Three Blind Mice") on a piece of wood wasn't going to give me an enriching life experience. So when they were both preoccupied doing things around the house, I snuck out and walked to the courthouse on Lombardy Road. I approached the most lawyerly looking man I saw. He was wearing a suit and carrying a briefcase and looked like he could get fast results. I told him I was interested in divorcing my parents and asked if he wanted to take on the case. He sat me down and said he couldn't. He said he was an attorney but he handled more criminal cases. I told him my parents were criminally insane but he said he doubted that. I was too smart to have been raised by crazy parents. He also said he couldn't take the case because he has a daughter a year or two older than me, and he made the mistake of leaving her and has regretted it ever since. He said I should take my time and think about if that's what I really want. Then he gave me his card and said to call him if I ever needed real help. He wanted to make sure I got back safe so he sent me home with a police escort. Mom and Dad were more embarrassed than upset when I pulled up to the house in the back of a police cruiser.

In any case, I plan to make this journal very detailed, in case it's ever entered into evidence. Then I'll call Ruben. I heard he's a district attorney now.

I should have brought him home with me that day so he could see for himself that the only thing missing in this house is Rod Serling. He'd be right at home sitting on a stool in our living room, able to jump up at a moment's notice to begin his intro to *The Twilight Zone: Juergens Family Edition*. He seems like the only one who would be able to put my thoughts into just the right context:

> *"Imagine if you will a family where the only sane person is a thirteen-year-old girl. She wakes up one morning to find she has reached a high level of maturity. Higher even than that of her parents, who insist on controlling her life through unreasonable rules and regulations. She has no one to turn to, not even her sister. It is here that she is forced to live in what can only be described as a teenage hell, and forced to fend for herself . . . in the Twilight Zone."*

If this really were possible then I'm sure my mom would do something completely embarrassing, like ask Rod to please put out his cigarette, and my dad would say something like, as long as there's no sex in the Twilight Zone I can stay as long as I want. I watched another *Twilight Zone* marathon the other weekend and the scariest thing about that show is how much sense it makes. And it made me jealous of the kid who can wish people into the cornfield.

10:18 P.M.

Amy was in a very good mood after Ben dropped her off. I've seen Amy this happy only when she made the high school marching band and when she found out that cute drummer, Ricky, was also going to band camp.

Her date with Ben couldn't have been that good. It was a football game followed by a Christian dance. All I heard from her was they had really good food and she danced with Ben. She talked about all the different kinds of food she ate for like ten minutes straight and spent maybe thirty seconds telling me about slow dancing with Ben. She even missed the one interesting thing that did happen at the dance. That majorette Adrian kissed Grace's boyfriend, Jack, and the whole school saw because Grace's brother Tom busted them. At least, that's what I overheard Madison and Lauren telling Amy in her room. Those two are annoying, but at least they know right away when something interesting happens. Not that you couldn't tell something like that was going to happen just by watching Adrian at the football game. Guys like nice girls? Yeah, right. So I was RIGHT and Dad was WRONG.

Then Lauren and Madison closed the door and I couldn't hear what they were talking about with Amy because they were whispering. Whatever they were saying . . . it sounded serious. I even thought I heard Amy crying at one point but I can't be sure because Mom caught me lingering in the hall and told me to go to bed and stop spying on Amy and her friends. She just wanted me out of the way so she could listen in.

Usually I don't get caught sneaking around like that. During the football game, when I couldn't take my dad talking about "nice" girls anymore, I excused myself to go to the bathroom and went looking for Ben's driver in the parking lot. He was pretty easy to spot. He was the only guy reading a book in the front seat of a town car. He rolled down the window and I apologized for bothering him, but I had a few questions about his employer's son. Sure, Amy and I don't have anything in common, don't understand each other, and fight sometimes, but she's still my sister. I have to make sure Ben is a nice guy. I asked the driver if Ben takes girls like Amy out all the time. He said not girls like Amy—not any girls actually. I asked if Ben's intentions toward Amy were honorable. He said they were. I asked if Ben had ever been in love. The driver said not before tonight. Ben sure moves fast. I told the driver to make sure no funny business went on in the backseat, and by funny business I meant sex. He said not to worry, so I wished him good night and left. When I got back to the bleachers my dad asked what took so long. I said there was a long line for the bathroom. See? I'm a pro.

When I got home from school the next day, Amy's mood, aka the pendulum, had swung to the other side. I don't even know what happened. My day was the same. School, boredom, Principal Miller gave me that smelly school sweatshirt again, I left it out by the basketball court, then I came home.

And the phone rang. That's when things took a turn for

the worse. It was that snob, Lauren, for Amy. I made sure to give her my best stink voice, then walked into Amy's room to hand her the phone like I always do, except this time she started yelling at me about barging in. She said she was upset about her privacy, but I think something else is going on. Amy doesn't really get mad. She's never yelled at me for walking into her room before. I'm always the one who gets annoyed, who complains about not having enough privacy, who tells everyone to mind their own business. At least she gave the same attitude over the phone to that snob Lauren. That was long overdue.

I know Amy pretty well. Not only because I live with her but also because of that stupid sisterly bond thing. I know something's up. And not because of the stuttering, the sweating, and the red face. I could have walked into her room backward and known she's not being the usual, boring Amy. I asked if it was because of Ben. She said it wasn't, but what else could it be?

My dad always said boys would make our lives more complicated. They are a slippery slope that would eventually lead to sex. Could Amy be having sex? I don't think so. I've heard you look different after you lose it. So I walked around Amy's room and looked at all of her pictures. There were the usual family pictures . . . boring. There were some with Lauren and Madison . . . whatever. Then there were a few from band camp—Amy waving good-bye after we dropped her off, her and another French horn player, and the day we picked her up from band camp. I compared the picture from the first day of band camp with the picture from the last day of band camp. Amy *did* look different. But maybe it was just the extra sun, the clean air, and being away from me and our parents. I told myself this was dumb. Amy looked the same, even after dating Ben. She might be a few pounds heavier, but maybe the "freshman fifteen" applies to high school, too.

Sept. 8th

On top of Amy's mood swings, I also have to deal with my parents—and not just about my clothes. I walked into the kitchen the other night and Mom and Dad were having a discussion about money. I've never heard them talk about money before. If this is the start of some kind of snowball effect, I'd hate to see the size of it by the time it rolls out the front door. Rod's going to get flattened in the middle of one of his monologues.

I think what started their fight was my mom worrying about our college funds. I told her I don't mind skipping high school, let alone college. Amy's been there a week and she's already unhappy. I figure you might as well be unhappy with all the comforts of home. I brought this up to my mom but she reminded me homeschooling involves her being around, too. Forget about that. As much as my dad can bug me sometimes, we do share a similar sense of humor. The only thing my mom and I agree on is that we don't understand each other. At all.

When I was little I was convinced I was adopted. I took some hair samples from my mom's hairbrush and mailed them to a genetic testing lab. They mailed the results back a few months later. The results said there was no doubt Anne Juergens was my mother. I had them redo the test two times until the head of the lab sent me a handwritten note assuring me the results were one hundred percent conclusive and asking me to please stop sending him my mother's hair. I've never trusted science since.

Sept. 13th

My mom asked me what's wrong with Amy. This made me nervous. If Mom is noticing that Amy's acting weird then this isn't just my imagination. I told her I didn't know. And for once, I really don't. Maybe it's this Ben guy. But he's so harmless. And besides dating Ben, nothing else has happened to Amy recently. Amy's life is so boring. The only thing she did all summer was go to band camp. I mean, how exciting can band camp be? Maybe if you decide you want to switch instruments or something?

Amy did just start high school, but I thought middle school was the new high school and high school the new college.

And college is just an extended vacation before actual life responsibilities. So really, she should be in the best mood ever, like she was yesterday.

Maybe I should ask Madison and Lauren. What am I saying? Even if they knew something they wouldn't tell me because we don't like each other, and if they didn't know anything they would start gossiping about what could be wrong with Amy. I could talk to Amy but she already yelled at me about her privacy. If she really wanted privacy she shouldn't make eavesdropping so easy.

8:22 P.M.

I overheard Amy talking to Ben tonight. I think I know what's going on now because I overheard her tell him she loved him, too. Her hormones must be going crazy. Love already? No way. Tomorrow she'll be sobbing and ignoring him at school. Unless it really is love, but . . .

Isn't love supposed to make you happy? Because Amy's definitely not happy. Neither are my parents. And I know I'm loved, but I wouldn't exactly call myself happy either. I smell a conspiracy brewing here.

Maybe that's why my dad's so afraid Amy and I will have sex. Because most teenagers have already figured out that love equals unhappiness, so why not just skip ahead to the fun stuff? Makes sense to me. I hope my dad doesn't find this journal anytime soon. I don't think he'd like the fact that I'm figuring out the truth on my own. The other night Mom almost sat on my journal when she came in to say good

The only thing that does make me happy is going by my own dress code—are you reading this, Principal Miller?!

night. She sat on my bed to talk and I could see the corner poke out from the duvet. I think I'll start hiding it in my air-conditioning vent. And then move it around to a new spot every couple of weeks just in case.

Sept. 16th

7:05 A.M.

Okay, Amy's mood is starting to rub off on me. She cut in front of me when it was my turn to use the bathroom. She's worse than Dad. I tried to hold her off but she brought up her privacy again and then shut the door in my face. Well, I need privacy, too. And I actually had some time-allotted privacy already set aside so I could get ready for school that she intruded on. I tried to use one of the other two bathrooms but Mom and Dad had already staked their claims. So I went back and sat outside the other bathroom and waited for Amy to come out.

I actually felt kind of bad for Amy because it sounded like she was throwing up. Could it be something she ate? Dinner was twelve hours ago. I think food poisoning hits faster than that. Maybe the flu is going around. I wish Lauren and Madison would catch it. They call all the time now and when they visit they go straight into Amy's room and shut the door. I hate feeling unwelcome in my own house. I enjoy making others feel unwelcome.

When Amy finally came out of the bathroom I asked her if she was feeling sick and she just snapped at me. What's the big deal about feeling under the weather? She's not going to get yelled at for catching a cold or grounded for having the flu. What is going on around here? What is she hiding? Why is this all I can think about lately? Should I still respect Amy's privacy when it intrudes on other people's lives, mainly mine?

The answer is obviously "no," but I have to fill up space in this thing somehow because Principal Miller said I have to write a certain number of pages a week.

So on that note . . . I haven't explained yet why I wasn't sent to camp this past summer. Now is as good a time as any. The reason is I've been banned from almost all of them:

Wilderness Appreciation Camp: I appreciate the wilderness enough to know I don't want to camp out there for weeks at a time. Last summer, I cabbed it to the local hotel after everyone was settled in their tents. My counselors warned me that if I did it one more time I would be sent home. They must not have realized I DID want to be sent home. So I did it one more time.

Animal Lovers Camp: This should have been called "Bug Lovers Camp." We rarely saw any actual animals and when we did they were either bugs or mosquitoes. I was constantly reminding them there actually is a place for animal lovers that is much more fun. It's called the zoo.

Science Camp: It's summer. And I'm at school during the summer because . . . ? And I already mentioned I don't trust science. I did try to genetically test my mom's hair on the first day but they lacked the proper equipment and the results were inconclusive. Some science camp.

Theater Camp: They claimed I was too dramatic. The final straw occurred when we performed *Hamlet.* I was cast as Ophelia and kept insisting she would have killed herself way earlier in the play. I was sent home and the part was recast. I don't even want to think how much the final show suffered because of my absence.

Band Camp: I don't play an instrument and they had already heard about me from the other camps. Who knew these people actually got together during the off-season? Plus, I've already shared my unfortunate history with the recorder.

And, believe it or not . . .

Girl Scouts: While all the other girls actually earned their badges, I found the store that sold them to all of the troop leaders and bought mine direct. At least I earned the money I bought the badges with by doing chores around the house. Doing chores doesn't have a badge, so if anything I'm actually owed one. My dad was very proud of me. Not only because I found a way to accumulate badges without actually earning them, but also because I got the badges wholesale. I should just be glad they didn't find out about all the stuff I pulled when I was a Brownie.

So that's why I spent my summer vacation at home watching TV. I loved it and can't wait to return next summer!

Sept. 18th

Amy's mood is now spreading to everyone in the family. Maybe it's a virus that puts you in a foul mood before shutting down your organs. Whatever it is, it's serious and highly contagious. My dad can't even stand to be in the house anymore. He makes any excuse to leave. He's working late at the furniture store or he's meeting an old friend for a drink or he's going for a walk. In truth, I don't think he's doing any of those things. I definitely know he's not at the furniture store because I called over there and all I got was his voice mail. Whatever he is doing, it isn't good. And I think Mom is starting to notice.

There's this tension between my parents that's thickened ever since they had that discussion about money. It's gotten to the point where every conversation between them is about money, even when they're talking about something else: "Beautiful day, isn't it, Anne?" "It would be if you would tell me where you're hiding all of our money, George." "Do you need me to pick up the girls after school, Anne?" "You can do that right after you tell me where our money went, George." "Good night, Anne." "Don't forget to turn out the light and let me know where you're keeping our money, George."

I know money isn't supposed to buy you happiness but it sure does a good job at keeping unhappiness at bay. My parents didn't fight this bad until they had money problems.

So when my mom asked if I wanted to go with her to the gas station, I practically skipped to the car. Anything to get out of our house. I thought it would just be a boring errand, but nothing is ever that simple when it comes to my family.

Dr. Hightower, our doctor, was there. I swear she flinched when she saw me.

I am not Dr. Hightower's favorite patient. Whenever I have a checkup she insists on asking me a million questions. And after each one I insist on asking, "Why do you want to know?" so my appointments usually run twice as long as the other patients'. We haven't been to see her in a while so the whole run-in was awkward.

Mom told her we don't feel comfortable going to see her since Dr. Bowman joined her practice. Dr. Marshall Bowman's current wife is Dad's ex-wife, Kathleen. It gets a little confusing because Kathleen and Marshall are Grace's parents. But in a town this small, there's bound to be some overlapping.

Dr. Hightower told my mom she'd get her a referral and told me that Amy and I are due for our school physicals. I'm surprised she brought this up since I usually mess up her schedule whenever I have an appointment. That reminded Mom that she got a doctor's bill for Amy even though she hadn't been to see Dr. Hightower. Dr. Hightower tried to act concerned, but it came across as more fake nice. Maybe she knew she was in a no-win situation with my mom. I can get that way, too, so I get it. It's just annoying when someone other than me does it.

4:00 P.M.

When I got home, Amy was trying on clothes in front of Madison and Lauren. I guess every day at Grant High School is a fashion show, but Amy doesn't have anything new. Maybe she should take Principal Miller's advice and layer, layer, layer!

Anyway, I think Madison and Lauren were both bored by Amy's fashion show, too, because when I walked in everyone was quiet. I gave Amy some tampons we got at the gas station because I knew she'd need them before I would. I left to join the tension downstairs because compared to Lauren and Madison, Mom and Dad are the lesser of two evils.

I, on the other hand, have endless amounts of creative outlets regarding clothes. Do you hear me, Principal Miller? I know you see me but do you HEAR me?

Weirdly, I noticed Madison had the box of tampons in her purse when she and Lauren were leaving. I asked Amy about it later and she stuttered that Madison was having a female emergency.

I told Amy we ran into Dr. Hightower at the gas station and Mom got a doctor's bill from her even though Amy hasn't had a checkup. Amy turned bright red and said she did go to see Dr. Hightower a few weeks ago for a school project. She had to write about someone she admires so she chose Dr. Hightower, and during the interview, Dr. Hightower went ahead and did a checkup.

Do I buy Amy's story? No way. Especially after I told her that Dr. Bowman just joined Dr. Hightower's practice. Her face went from red to white. I mean, we're not happy about Dr. Bowman being there but it's nothing to lose sleep over. I'm more concerned that Amy admires Dr. Hightower so much. Why????? The woman gets flustered when you ask her a question or twenty!

5:32 P.M.

While Amy was in the shower I snuck into her room to investigate. I flipped through her calendar looking for the red stars Amy always draws to keep track of her time of the month. I started in January. Amy usually gets it every thirty days, like clockwork. But as I got closer to the present I stopped seeing those stars. I hadn't seen them for over a month when I finally caught up to today's date. It doesn't necessarily mean anything. It could be the stress of starting a new school or all that extra marching Amy has to do during football games. . . .

I went over every scenario to try to figure out where those stars went. I was so stressed out over it I hardly touched my dinner. The good news is that Amy's mood hasn't affected her stomach. Her appetite is bigger than Dad's. It's kind of amazing. If they were to enter some kind of eating contest, I'd put money on Amy, hands down. She devoured the burgers Mom made for dinner and took a box of crackers to bed with her. I asked why and she said she was still hungry and didn't want to have to make the long walk to the kitchen in the middle of the night for a snack.

When I got to my room I went straight for my computer. Sherlock Holmes had Watson, I have Google. I entered all of Amy's symptoms and clicked on "search" even though I already pretty much knew what was going on.

At least, I think I do. But I can't believe I'm thinking it, even as I'm writing it down. Okay, there's one thing I like about this journal. When you are scared to even think something and you can't tell anyone, you can at least write it down and feel a little bit better.

At the same time, I can't believe I'm writing about a serious life topic in my journal. I'm so cliché.

I mean, it's all starting to make sense now, I guess.

Sept. 19th

Mom wanted to take Amy shopping to get some dating clothes. She must have noticed Amy's sad fashion show earlier with Madison and Lauren. I should tell Mom I'm dating someone and then I could get some new clothes, too. Amy insisted I come with them even though I just wanted to lie down and watch TV with Dad because he was actually home for once. She never insists I come anywhere.

When we were alone in the dressing room, Amy seemed to want to tell me something when Mom wasn't around. She'd look at me like she was about to say something but then . . . nothing. I got that same feeling when Amy called over the summer from band camp sounding so upset but insisted nothing was wrong. Then Mom came back with an armful of clothes for Amy to try on. Amy came out to model one outfit for Mom and I told her it was too baggy. Amy said it fit perfectly. She just stood there and stared at herself in the mirror, like she was in some kind of a daze. She snapped out of it when Mom mentioned her swollen feet and her curves. Amy immediately changed the subject.

That's when I told Mom I don't understand why she insists on covering me up but pushes Amy to flaunt everything she's got. I must admit it does seem like Amy grew a pair of boobs overnight. I don't know where those two came from but they are big. So are her feet. I don't remember band practice taking such a physical toll on Amy, but that French horn is kinda big and walking around with it all day must be hard on her feet and . . .

Oh, what am I saying? Marching in band may make your feet swell but it doesn't give you big boobs. If it did it would be the most popular extracurricular activity at school. I tried asking Amy about it a bunch of times, but each time I chickened out. It's like if I actually say the words, then it becomes real.

7:06 P.M.

When we got home, Mom and Dad started going at it. Figuratively, of course. Not going at it like in an actual fistfight, but more like a light slapping through words kind of thing. Like when two girls get in a fight during lunch and just circle each other. Dad wouldn't like the fact I'm comparing him to girls at my school, but that's what it reminded me of. I was suddenly jealous of Amy's date with Ben. I hate being at home when my parents are arguing.

I went into Amy's room to tell her Dad and I were going to get food. She was wearing one of the new tops she had just gotten at the mall and the way she was standing confirmed what I had feared.

And then I asked about her boobs.

I know what you're thinking, why didn't I ask if she was pregnant? I was working my way up to that question. I thought complimenting her on her boobs would help her open up. It didn't. She got defensive and said I was staring at her. I told her she's gotten kind of sexy lately. (Sexy as in had sex. Whoa, I really sounded like my dad there.) And now I'm experiencing his worst fear—Amy's pregnant. I didn't say that last part out loud. Amy shrugged me off and I couldn't think of another question, so I left with Dad.

During the car ride he brought up Mom and wondered if I knew what's put her in such a bad mood. I said I didn't know. I was just glad he hadn't noticed anything about Amy. To make sure we didn't get on the topic of Amy, I took a major conversational detour.

I looked at my dad and asked him if he had sex before marriage. He pulled the car over, turned off the engine, took off his seat belt, and looked at me. He wanted to know why I was asking. I said because I wanted to know and I wanted him to tell me the truth. He leaned back in his seat and sighed. "Let me preface this by saying, 'Do as I say and not as I do.' Yes, Ash. I had sex before I was married. But that doesn't give you carte blanche to do the same." I asked if he regretted it. He was taking his time, choosing his words very carefully. I told him I wasn't asking him these questions so I would have an excuse to go have sex. I was just curious. He said at the time he didn't regret having sex before marriage, but he regrets it now. I asked why and he said having Amy and me changed his mind. It made him think that it wasn't fair to the other girls (he told me not to get a crazy number in my head but wouldn't elaborate), who were also somebody's daughter, to be treated like that, like they weren't special. So if he had two sons instead of two daughters he wouldn't feel that way? Dad said yes. I told him that's a double standard and he said he couldn't help it; it's just different with guys. They don't get as emotionally involved as girls do. I told him I'm not emotional like most girls and he said emotional or not, I could still get preg-nant. I asked him if getting pregnant was the worst thing I could do. He said the worst thing I could do is have sex any-time soon. Then he started the car and we picked up din-ner. Dad kept looking at me out of the corner of his eye the whole time.

7:45 P.M.

When we got back Amy had already left for the fair with Ben. When she gets back I'm going to ask her if she's pregnant. Maybe hanging out with Ben will put her in a good mood and she'll be more open to talking to me.

I cornered Mom while she was brushing her teeth and asked if she had sex before she was married. Mom sighed and I said I know, do as you say and not as you do. Mom said as long as that's clear, then yes, she did have sex before she was married. I told her not to worry; I wouldn't run out and have sex just because she told me the truth. I'm not a follower. I didn't ask if she regretted it. Living her whole life having had sex only with Dad? That she would probably regret.

10:20 P.M.

I did it.

No, not that. I asked Amy. I waited up for her on the couch. Mom and Dad didn't even notice me pacing around the living room because they were too busy bickering. Amy got home earlier than I expected because she got sick on the carousel. Amy loves the carousel. And she normally has a pretty strong stomach.

Oh no. Why do all signs keep pointing to yes?

I knew I was right even before she answered. I told her she

needed a friend in the house and that I would keep her secret. I cried and I'm not a big crier. I think the last time I cried was during some cheesy romance movie that was so bad I couldn't believe it had been made, but I actually sat through two whole hours watching it and weeping. I think seeing me cry made Amy realize how serious her situation is. But I didn't cry because Amy is pregnant. I cried because even though Amy and I have our differences, I thought we were friends. I wish she had confided in me instead of calling Madison and Lauren and shutting the door and whispering with them in her room. She didn't tell me her secret on her own. I had to ask her. And that really hurt. But I guess that doesn't matter now. I'm still her sister and her friend, even if she didn't really realize it until now.

And I know the perfect way to help her.

10:42 P.M.

Ben just left. He came back to return Amy's jacket. She forgot it in the middle of all the puking. He told her he loved her and then left. I asked if he knows she's pregnant. She said he doesn't know. At least I wasn't the only one who was left in the dark, besides Mom and Dad.

Ben must really love Amy a lot. He kissed her even after she had puked right in front of him. Wow. But there's something that's bothering me. Amy and Ben just started dating. I don't know how far along Amy is but it just doesn't seem to click. On the other hand, Amy hasn't dated anyone else, unless something happened over the summer. But nothing happened over the summer.

Amy just went to band camp.

Sept. 20th

7:12 A.M.

I must have spent at least an hour digging around my closet for something to wear today. I was worried I didn't have anything, but then I found some stuff at the back that I had been saving for Halloween. I figured if I was going to distract Mom and Dad from Amy's behavior, then I really needed to do something crazy to get everyone's attention. And, let's be honest, driving my parents nuts is just an added bonus.

Like a couple of years ago when I sat outside the house in a foldout chair holding a sign that said PROTEST AGAINST PARENTS. The neighborhood got really mad when all the

This was the outfit you complimented me on, Principal Miller. You said I was really starting to understand what dressing appropriately for school meant. That was also the last time you ever saw that outfit because it went straight to the back of the closet after I got home from school. I don't think I will wear it for Halloween. I already scared my parents.

other kids joined me. It allowed me to take bathroom breaks without undermining the seriousness of the protest. Or when Dad made me work in the furniture store because he wanted me to go into the family business and I told all the customers how much the store's markup actually was. Ahhh, memories. But I think this will be my masterpiece.

It worked immediately. Right when I walked into the kitchen wearing a long black skirt, ruffled shirt, and black sweater my dad asked me what was going on. I'm trying to remember the last time I was so covered up. It must have been in kindergarten or something. I mean we're talking *layers* here. Your favorite word, Principal Miller.

I was planning on being a nun for Halloween. Or a secretary.

My demure outfit wasn't exactly newsworthy, but it led my mom and dad to believe I was having sex. They thought I was covering up the fact I was having sex by actually, literally covering up. This was not the response I was expecting. I guess some customer at my dad's store heard a rumor that a Juergens girl was having sex and they just assumed it was me. They're not even thinking it could be Amy. Good. For added

Before I spooked my dad with my outfit, he was in a very good mood because of news footage of Grace being shown on TV. I don't think he would have cared as much if it hadn't been his ex-wife's daughter. I guess Grace was out really late and had to defend herself against a couple of guys who started bugging her, when that drummer Ricky came to her rescue out of nowhere and hugged her... without a shirt. And it was all caught on camera. Wow, I can see why Amy was so excited to see him at band camp. Maybe the recorder isn't so bad.... See, wardrobe (or lack thereof) is an excellent way to get attention. In this case it was even newsworthy.

effect I gave a shout-out to my lover and undid my prim hairstyle. The looks on Mom's and Dad's faces were priceless. I wanted to enjoy it a little bit longer but my job was done, so I made sure the top button on my blouse was buttoned and left for school.

That's another good thing about being a distraction. Me dressing up and fueling a rumor that couldn't possibly be about Amy keeps them occupied, so they are talking to each other without fighting. I think Mom's concerns about money have Dad freaked out and that's why he's working longer hours at the store. Who knows? All I know is I'd rather have them stand there and accuse me of having sex than ask me if something is up with Amy or fight about money.

This isn't the first time I've covered for Amy. Nothing as serious as a pregnancy, but still, if my parents knew, they'd be surprised. Like the time I got in a fight at school. It was really Amy. Well, it was more like a kid was starting a fight with Amy, so I stepped in and punched him. I should probably get ready to defend Amy's honor over and over from now on.

6:32 P.M.

All my hard work almost went down the toilet today. Amy told Dad I'm not the one having sex, she is. I ran in and acted like Amy was crazy. My parents didn't believe her anyway. Then they took a break to fight with each other. Great, I wore an outfit all day that made it look like I was allergic to the sun and they don't believe the truth when it's told to them? I didn't need to go through the trouble. My mom's enough of a distraction for my dad and Amy couldn't be a distraction even if she wanted to.

I told Amy not to tell them. With everything going on, we don't need to add a baby to the mix. Well, I mean, it's already in the mix but my parents don't need to know that. I asked Amy if Ben knows yet. She said he doesn't. She asked if she should tell him. (NOOOOOOOOOOOOOOOOOOOOO!) I told her I'm not old enough to give out that kind of advice. Even though I'm dressed like I'm mature and boring (for the time being), it's just a front.

I wanted to ask Amy how far along she is. It's been bothering me because I've been doing the math in my head, and the more I think about it the more I think Ben doesn't have anything to do with this baby. I remembered that stupid football game my parents made me go to and how Amy couldn't stop staring at Ricky, the guy she had a crush on, the guy she was so excited to see at band camp.

I think Ricky's the father of Amy's baby.

Sept. 22nd

My dad's going to Vegas. This worries me. Not because I actually know what he's like when he's in Vegas but because I think he's lying. First it's late nights at the furniture store. Then it's playing pool. Now it's Vegas.

I don't want to talk about this anymore.

Okay, I do want to talk about this some more. Because I know he's lying about it. I confronted him, too. I asked if Mom kicked him out and if he's seeing someone else. He said he wasn't but I don't believe him. My dad's not a loner. If he's not at home with his family he's with someone else. But he wouldn't admit it. He told me this isn't the type of stuff a dad talks about with his daughter. He will go on and on about my sex life but he will not admit he's cheating on Mom. He always dodges my questions like this when I'm right. I don't want to be right. Not now. Not again. The last time I was right was when I thought Amy might be pregnant. Then I had a hunch Ricky was the father. Last night, Amy admitted she had sex with Ricky at band camp and he is the father of her baby. Now I have a feeling Mom and Dad will probably get divorced, which will complete the family trifecta.

I also don't want the only parent I see every day to be my mom. I know that sounds harsh, but it's true. She doesn't understand me like Dad does. Once Amy's secret comes out, I'll need Dad here. Because even though Mom and Dad aren't getting along right now, they balance each other out. And this situation needs balance.

Since I already knew the bad news, my only other option was to try to change it. I asked him not to leave. He told me since I'm always acting older, I should be able to handle the fact that things don't always happen the way you want them to. I've realized this a lot. Especially lately. But I'd like to meet the person who actually handles disappointment well and see how old they are. It's probably someone way younger than me who isn't even old enough to understand what's being told to them.

My dad wouldn't budge, so I started bargaining with him. If he promised not to leave, I would wear whatever he wanted me to wear. I would even wear that gross sweatshirt you gave me, Principal Miller. (I'd have to go find it by the cafeteria, but I'd wear it when I found it.) I'd get good grades and act genuinely interested in school and I'd try not to be such a loner and make some friends. Not friends like Lauren and Madison, though.

I even CRIED AGAIN. I really hate that this crying thing has started to become a regular occurrence. But I couldn't help it. And I told him that. I knew things were bad when the crying didn't change anything. I thought it would do the trick. It certainly freaked Amy out. I even considered showing him this journal. But I'm starting to get attached to it. It's like my safety blanket. That sounds so unlike me but it's true.

Dad tried to make it better by saying he'd always be around. I hate when parents lie and know they're lying. Since when do you pack a suitcase to be around? You don't. You pack it when you're leaving. How am I supposed to trust he'll be around when he can't even be honest about where he's actually going? Vegas, my butt.

At that point I wanted to tell him about Amy and the baby so badly. That would have stopped him from walking out. But I promised Amy she could trust me as a friend. And I don't want her not to trust me anymore. Amy really needs me right now. More than I need my dad.

They're going to get divorced. I know it. Dad says it's just a break. But "break" is code for "breakup." It just means the people involved don't have the guts to call it what it is yet.

And now I'll have another thing in common with all the kids at my school. Divorced parents. I better fish my protest sign out of the garage and go sit out on the lawn again.

My dad's parting words to me? Things happen. Yeah, I know things happen. That doesn't mean you have to sit there, or in his case walk out, and let them happen. He didn't have to cheat on Mom and he doesn't have to leave. I'd like to hear Amy say that to him after she tells him she's pregnant and see him accept it like I'm forced to now. This separation thing didn't have to happen. Dad didn't have to be out every night. That just made things worse.

I don't like school but I still show up every day. I get through it.

Sorry Principal Miller, but you know it's true.

My mom heard me yell after my dad that he shouldn't leave, especially now. She wondered what I meant by that. Whoops. I told her it's hard to have a parent leave when you're my age and Amy's age.

Because that's kind of the truth, too.

When Amy and I were younger our parents didn't fight like this. They had a rule similar to "never go to bed angry" except it was "never go to bed angry unless the other person's being a moron." Dad was usually the moron in that scenario. They'd eventually end up laughing, with Dad admitting he was a moron and Mom telling him she loved him because he was a moron. But this time they haven't ended up laughing and no one's admitting they're a moron.

6:48 P.M.

Amy came home and told me she's getting married. Exactly how many secrets am I supposed to keep at one time? Here's the tally so far: Amy's pregnant (keep this secret from Mom and Dad and basically everyone), Ricky's the father (keep this secret from Mom and Dad and Ben), Mom and Dad are probably getting a divorce (keep this secret from Amy . . . and me—it's too painful to fully acknowledge at the moment), and Amy and Ben are getting married (don't tell Mom and Dad).

I told Amy marriage was a bad idea given that she's only fifteen, but Amy corrected me by saying she's fifteen and pregnant. I wanted to tell her first comes love, then comes marriage, then comes the baby in the baby carriage, but I bit my tongue. I didn't want my sarcasm to hurt the baby's feelings, and besides, marriage ends up being a bad idea for lots of people at all ages. Not just fifteen.

She did tell me Ben's dad knows she's pregnant so everyone will know soon enough—one less secret.

I started thinking back to simpler times, when Amy was boring and I had no secrets to keep. I remember one time she had Lauren and Madison over for a sleepover and I hid in the closet to witness their lameness in action. They decided to play the "Never have I ever . . ." game. The players hold up ten fingers and go around the room saying things they have never done. If another player has done it, they put one of their fingers down. The game ends when someone has all ten fingers down. Amy, Lauren, and Madison started playing and every statement had to be related to sex. Lauren started, "Never have I ever . . . kissed a boy." Amy and Madison looked at each other, all fingers still up. Needless to say, if you haven't kissed a boy the game's pretty much over. They ended up saying things like, "Never have I ever . . . water-skied." The game finally ended when I shouted from inside the closet, "Never have I ever been so bored in my life!" I remember thinking, as Amy threw me out of her room, how I wished my sister wasn't so boring. The good news is she can now hold her own the next time anyone wants to play "Never have I ever . . ."

Amy wants to tell Mom she's pregnant but I told her she's got some time. Mom's clueless for the moment because she's preoccupied with Dad leaving, something Amy already knew about. I wish Amy would let me in on things a little sooner. Maybe I could have avoided crying again and tried talking to Dad earlier. Then I could have stopped him from leaving.

She did get me laughing when she said, Who would want to have sex with Dad if they didn't have to? Seriously. I don't know why I suddenly stopped seeing the funny side of things, and who would have thought Amy would be the one to set me straight? It didn't take her long to start crying, though. She doesn't think she can keep the baby.

Great. Another secret.

Sept. 23rd

7:02 A.M.

I woke up this morning thinking it was just another day. Well, another day as in pretending Amy's not pregnant and Mom and Dad aren't getting divorced. Because, let's face it, that's what normal is now. Or at least I thought it was until I walked into the kitchen.

Amy told Mom about the baby. I know Mom had to find out at some point but I would have appreciated a heads-up. I walked right into a trap. I came in for breakfast and left in almost as much trouble as Amy. I was actually glad for a second Dad wasn't there.

Mom asked me if I knew. I tried *I can handle a lot.*
to cover but Amy ratted me out. I *It's not just for show.*
was ready to keep her secret for nine months and she sold
me out in nine seconds. I went down swinging, though. I said
maybe Amy's pregnancy was the result of an alien abduction.
Mom was not amused and cut me off before I could run down
my list of other possible scenarios: Immaculate Conception,
food baby, gas, or high school biology project gone horribly
wrong.

Before Mom could focus on me, Amy told her she wanted
to get an abortion. That's when Mom sent me to my room.
She must have thought I couldn't handle the conversation.

I didn't want to tell her Amy and I had already talked about
that last night. . . .

I couldn't sleep and went into Amy's room to talk. I hadn't
planned on going in there to talk about anything. I had been
tossing and turning for a couple of hours with Amy and the
baby on my mind. I knew *The War of the Roses* was going to be
on TV soon and I figured it would make me feel better about
Mom and Dad's situation, so I walked down the hall toward
the living room. Amy saw me walk past her door and called
me into her room because she was up, too. Her voice didn't
sound tired or anything. I was surprised she was awake. Out
of all the times I've gotten up to watch a movie in the middle
of the night, this is the first time she's been awake and called
me into her room. All that privacy must be getting to her.

I sat at the end of her bed and we talked about how quiet

the house is with Dad gone. Usually when Mom and Dad fight he ends up on the couch and watches movies with me, but since he's not here I'm left to make the popcorn and Juergens commentary by myself. It's just not the same. Commercial breaks are more fun with Dad there.

All of a sudden Amy asked if I would think less of her if she had an abortion. I looked down, ashamed for complaining all the time. I never realized how fantastic my problems are. So fantastic they aren't even problems compared to what Amy has to worry about. I told Amy I meant what I said before, about being her friend, and that I would support her in whatever she decides to do. But deep down, I hope she doesn't get an abortion. But I didn't tell her that. That's why it's probably a good thing Amy finally told Mom about the baby. Because even though I'm Amy's sister and friend, the person she really needs now is Mom.

I told her getting an abortion is a big decision. A decision best not made in the middle of the night by two sisters whose minds are so busy and confused that they aren't allowing them to sleep. Amy agreed but said it also wasn't a decision that can wait for very long because decisions only get harder the longer you wait to make them. She had me there. I suggested weighing all of her options before thinking about that, and one of those options would be to tell Mom and Dad about this and see what they think.

She said telling them she was pregnant was going to be hard enough . . . now this? I told Amy I've had to tell Mom and Dad lots of stuff and it's not so bad. Like the time I tried to drive myself to school. Sure, the yelling can get loud and punishments aren't fun (although I don't think any punishment can outlast the nine months she's currently serving) but then it's over and you get that small break before the next lockdown. You get used to it. Amy looked at me and told me she didn't think she could get used to any of this. She had me there. Again.

Why is it that I used to be the one making the points and being right? It was only after this past summer all that changed. Now that Amy's pregnant she's turned into some kind of sage or something. Where was this person during band camp when this whole mess started?

I decided not to bring that up. I mean, if we all had the option to go back in time then I think time travel would be as normal an occurrence as going to the bathroom. But sometimes mistakes need to be made in order for you to realize they actually weren't mistakes in the first place. That's why I don't think Amy should get an abortion. I told Amy we should sleep on all this for now because I was getting tired, so Amy and I went back to bed. Or at least I thought Amy had gone to bed. I had no idea she had planned on waiting up all night in the kitchen for Mom.

I left the kitchen to let Mom and Amy talk. Amy must be so tired of talking by now. I know I am. I went upstairs, but not to my room. I went into Amy's. I don't even know why, and it's not because I could hear them in the kitchen better. It was because even though a lot of things have changed lately, Amy's room hasn't. Not in five years. So being in there made it seem like Amy wasn't pregnant, Dad was living here, and a certain conversation wasn't going on in the kitchen.

My room's a little bipolar . . . it changes every couple of months. Right now it has a kind of *Beetlejuice* aesthetic. But nothing about me is really different from five years ago.

Weird.

Later, I went back into the kitchen to see if I should be making any attempt to get ready for school. Mom told me I wasn't going to school. I didn't think we'd all be going underground. I think my mom told you I was sick, Principal Miller, or somebody died or something. I'm assuming since it was my mom who lied to you that means I won't get in trouble for skipping school. And if I do get in trouble so long after the fact . . . just take it up with my mother.

I asked if that was my punishment for not telling anyone about the baby. She told me I should have come to her and said Amy was in trouble. The same could be said for her marriage—which I told her—and that got me pulled into the hallway right away. She said I blame her for Dad leaving. I don't—I blame them both. But since she's here and wants to talk about it, then yes, the focus is on her right now. They both could have done something to help their marriage, but they didn't, and now we all have to deal with that on top of Amy's pregnancy. She didn't speak up when she sensed trouble either. Like mother, like daughter. I was going to thank her for the master class in irony but thought better of it— I'm in enough trouble as it is and I haven't even had breakfast yet.

I told her I didn't want Amy to go away like Dad. I needed her here. She's all I have in this house. I could tell I hurt Mom's feelings, but she's closer to Amy, like I am with Dad. I'm surprised she wants to send Amy away and be trapped in this house with just me. I should have told her I would have felt the same way if she was the one who left and Dad stayed. This house is different when we're not all together.

I know I said before I had the best summer ever because Amy wasn't here and I was by myself. But that's because I always knew she was coming back. I don't think my dad's coming back. And I don't want Amy leaving if she's not returning.

I tried to change her mind about Amy going to our grandmother's house. Mimsy's is a place we go for fun visits and vacations, not to hide out. But she doesn't think Amy can stay here with everyone knowing she's pregnant. I broke the news to her that everyone already knows Amy's pregnant: Lauren and Madison, Dad's customers, Ben, Ben's dad, everyone at Amy's high school, everyone at my school, me, insert your name here.

She and Dad were the only ones who didn't know.

Amy and I stayed pretty close to each other after that bombshell breakfast. The only time we do that is when one of us is sick. I try to catch whatever Amy has so I can get sick and stay home from school, or Amy tries to catch whatever I have to just get it over with. You can't catch pregnancy, though, although Dad has tried to scare us into thinking if we stand close enough to a boy, anything's possible. And unfortunately for Amy, you can't just get it over with.

Is this what life is going to be like with Dad now? Cell phone calls to make sure we've brushed our teeth and are going to bed on time? Is he going to be on speaker phone during family meetings? Do Amy and I need to get a special calling plan for fighting parents?

Speaking of my dad, he called Amy on her cell phone to see what's going on over here.

Amy tried to act like everything was okay, but started crying. Mom grabbed the phone and ended up being the one to tell Dad that Amy's pregnant. I have no idea what Dad's reaction to the news was, but I have a feeling it sounded something like this:

CRICKETS............CRICKETS............CRICKETS............

Mom took Amy's phone with her to avoid any more breakdowns from Amy. So much for the calling plan.

Would you think less of me, Principal Miller, if I told you I hoped this news would make my dad move back home? My belly button doesn't seem so terrible now, does it?

My phone rang and I knew it was either Madison or Lauren because the caller ID said: AMY'S LOSER FRIEND . . . I had a fifty-fifty shot of being right but a one hundred percent shot at being annoyed. Turns out it was both of them calling on the same line. They tried to act concerned about Amy, but all they're ever concerned about is themselves. I wish Amy would find better friends. Just because you've been friends with someone for a long time doesn't mean you have to keep being their friend. And they're the ones who told everyone at school Amy was pregnant. They're the reason she wants to go live with Mimsy. They wanted me to give her a message, but I hung up on them instead. They probably weren't surprised—it wasn't the first time. But I was too mad to tell them what I really thought. I should have told Lauren she's a snob and will probably stop coming over here once she feels the stigma of having a pregnant friend, and I should have told Madison I know she's just calling because she wants the latest scoop so she can blab about it all over school.

I once tried to prove to Amy that her friends couldn't be trusted. I told them Amy was dropping out of school to play her French horn on the street for spare change. It took only a half hour for people to start calling Amy to ask her which street corner she would be working on.

Even though no one needs to be reminded, I'm going to do it anyway: these are the two people she chose to confide in first. And this will not be the last time I hang up on them.

I did tell Amy they called. Luckily, she didn't call them back but instead wanted that girl Adrian's number. Amy must be the only person in school who doesn't have her number. I bet Adrian would be good at the "Never have I ever . . ." game. Amy wouldn't tell me why she needed to call her (I hope it wasn't for sex advice) but she did say all the secrecy was for my own good and because she does trust me. And since other people know she trusts me, they'll ask me where she's going. I just wanted to know if she was coming back.

I don't really care where she's going as long as she's coming back.

Mom walked in and we asked her about Dad. She said he's probably out looking for Ben. How could I not realize that would happen? A boy once made me cry in third grade (the only time that's happened and it was because he told me he had a crush on me) and Dad hunted him down at his own birthday party and made him apologize before he let him eat a bite of cake. I don't even want to think about what he's going to do to Ben. I think Mom could read my face because she told me to tell her anything else she should know. I quickly ran down the list in my head: the father of Amy's baby is Ricky, not Ben; Dad is having an affair; and Amy's going to sneak out of the house the first chance she gets.

I decided to tell her the first secret. The poor woman's had a rough morning. As soon as I told her Ben wasn't the father, she called Dad to let him know, and so the innocent stayed safe and all possible and metaphorical cake-eating was uninterrupted. Apparently Dad had almost made it to Ben's homeroom when he had to turn back. The thought of Ben's squeaky voice trying to calm my dad down ("No, no, Mr. Juergens, you've got it all wrong!") has been very entertaining.

While Mom was on the phone, I helped Amy climb out the window. I've never needed help climbing out the window. It's not that high and with a little "mind over matter" mentality it can go quite quickly. With the way Amy's year has gone so far, I'm sure she'll master it in no time.

I climb out the window only when I need time to myself . . . and to avoid my mother.

I still don't know where Amy's going. All I know is Ben and Adrian picked her up. She told me she loved me. It surprised me and scared me at the same time. Did that mean she wasn't coming back? It was more like a good-bye "I love you" than an "I'm just reminding you that I love you." It's the same tone Dad used right before he left with his suitcase. I told her to just go. What I really meant was "Just go but please come back." She's the only one around here who treats me like an adult.

Please come back, Amy.

I told Mom that Amy was in the bathroom, which at this point—given all the crying and drama and morning sickness—was very believable. I asked if she was going to let Amy marry Ben. She said they're too young. I can't believe Amy's even thinking of marriage after witnessing Mom's and Dad's behavior recently. I mean, Ben seems like a nice guy—he wants to be with Amy even though it's not his baby—but I'm sure Mom didn't think any of this would ever happen with Dad when they got married. And Mom wasn't even pregnant with another guy's baby. It just all seems so complicated. Could marriage possibly uncomplicate it? What am I even saying? I think I'm hearing *The Twilight Zone* theme music again. Cue Rod:

"Picture if you can a world where the institution of marriage isn't so much a destination but an escape. An escape from your worries and problems until you discover that your loving partner has become your worst enemy, to have and to hold until death do you part. Throw a baby into the mix and you have the exact reason Ashley Juergens is choosing to live the single life in . . . the Twilight Zone."

2:37 P.M.

MY DAD WANTS TO COME HOME! MY DAD WANTS TO COME HOME! MY DAD WANTS TO COME HOME!

I overheard him telling Mom. Obviously, she's not thrilled and doesn't really want him back here, but at least he wants to come home. He also wanted to find out from me how Amy ended up having sex and getting pregnant despite his constant warnings. I broke it down for him:

AMY + BAND CAMP − FRENCH HORN + RICKY + 2½ MINUTES − CONDOM = PREGNANT

(See, I *was* paying attention in math class.) I also told him that Ricky has a girlfriend named Adrian. Out of everything I told him that seemed to bother him the most. Umm, why? He doesn't even know this girl, so why would he care so much?

Why am I even worrying about it? I have too much to think about already. Dad also asked if Mom was seeing anybody. Jealousy isn't usually good in a relationship, but it's good in this case. Maybe if he's jealous he'll want to move back for good.

I told him she's seeing ten other guys. Okay, I didn't. I wanted to and I came very close, but I didn't.

3:32 P.M.

Amy came back with Mom. She went to go "take care of it," as they say, but ended up changing her mind. She didn't want to talk about it. I know Amy didn't tell me where she was going in order to protect me, but I wish she had. I could have gone with her, supported her. But I didn't take it personally because she came back home, she told me she had decided to keep the baby—and Dad's home, at least for a little while.

7:12 P.M.

Amy and Mom were talking in the kitchen tonight. I couldn't hear what they were saying, but it sounded like a nice talk.

That must mean Amy will be talking to Mom more about everything. That's good. It'll cut down on the window escapes.

And Amy probably got the first good night's sleep she's had in a long time.

Sept. 25th

7:55 A.M.

You can't make jokes in this house. Which is too bad for me and really bad for my dad—well, I mean if he still lived here it would be too bad for him. I make a little joke about how even though I'm late for school at least I'm not late for my period, and my mom forces me to apologize to Amy. At least I'm trying to find humor in the situation. Most people can't even do that . . . like my mom. And any sense of humor she might have had has been obliterated completely by Babygate. So with sarcasm and humor not allowed, I might have to become a mime with no personality. It's good I have this journal. I can communicate with the world somehow.

I started talking seriously about Dad coming home to help. That wasn't received well, either. Amy said she's not even going to be staying here. Then she stormed off. My mom said she thought we were getting along. So did I. But every day seems to be different around here. One day I'm helping her escape out the window, the next she's barely speaking to me. That's why I thought it was a good time to bring up Dad, since I'm not the only one not getting along with people. But it seems like it's never a good time to bring up Dad. My mom still wanted to talk about Amy, which I am sick of doing. I want to talk about Dad, about him moving back into the house, back where he belongs. I'm fine with Mom being serious about everything as long as Dad's here to counteract it with his sense of humor—it might be lame, but at least it's something. And let's face it, I wouldn't mind apologizing for stuff if there was someone next to me being made to apologize, too.

I wonder where Dad is. I don't think he went to Vegas; I think he's still in town but I don't know where. I called all of the local hotels and there wasn't a George Juergens staying in any of them.

If Amy's really leaving then he has to come back—the idea of me and Mom trapped in this house together is just too depressing. And if that's not going to happen then I might as well pack up my stuff and leave, too. I can go live with my dad wherever he's living, as long as it isn't with his mistress. I told this to my mom minus the mistress part. She changed the subject but didn't say no.

8:32 A.M.

School seemed even more ridiculous than usual with all this stuff going on at home. Plus, everyone has brothers and sisters who go to Amy's school and know she's pregnant, thanks to Lauren and Madison. I stayed at school for only ten minutes before I couldn't take it anymore and left.

Principal Miller, this detention should be removed from my record for the following reasons: number of pitying glances received from fellow students: 13; number of teachers/administrators who asked me to give them the scoop on Amy: 5 (4 if we don't count you, Principal Miller); number of students who tried to start inane conversations with me in the hopes I would bring up Amy and the baby: 11; number of times the crowded hallway parted like the Red Sea every time I came around a corner: 2. That is if you are even reading this, which I really doubt. I know this journal is at the bottom of a pile somewhere in a school closet where no one will find it until the next principal comes along. Which is kind of too bad. There's juicy stuff in here.

8:42 A.M.

I started walking home when the bag boy from the grocery store drove by and gave me a ride. He's kind of obsessed with me, which is usually annoying but convenient today. I think his name is Ned . . . or maybe it's Ted. Anyway, whenever NedTed bags our groceries he stares at me instead of focusing on what he's doing. He must have broken five dozen of our eggs since he started working there. He also bags our groceries using both paper and plastic. I think in his mind that's the equivalent of giving me a dozen roses or something.

As NedTed drove me home he made small talk by telling me what was currently on special (artichokes and tomato sauce, if you're interested). I think he could tell I was getting bored because I kept trying to turn up the radio. He asked if Amy went to school with a girl named Adrian. I said yeah. He said she's in the grocery store buying condoms all the time. Then he told me he liked my outfit.

Another one of your favorites, Principal Miller—my red plaid kilt miniskirt with my favorite skull-and-bones tee, remember? I think it's landed me into detention a few times before.

When I got home, I was relieved to see that Amy was still around. I asked her about Dad, because I figured she had talked to him and I knew she wouldn't get upset or avoid the question like Mom. She said Dad wants to come home (YES!) but Mom won't let him (NO!), so that's pretty much where things still stand at this point.

No wonder she was your favorite, Principal Miller.

Amy asked if I was worried about getting in trouble for skipping school.

Yeah, me skipping school > pregnancy and Dad moving out. With a little help from me, Amy realized

I just realized NedTed knows where I live now. This is very unfortunate.

how ridiculous she sounded. This is rare. I thanked her for being the ultimate distraction, but then remembered I've kind of been a distraction for her since I was born. . . . Well, at least I would have been if Amy had ever done anything before that warranted a distraction.

I told her she's taking this whole moping around thing to the extreme. She's not dying, she's pregnant. I didn't tell her this because I don't support her. I do support her. Completely. She's just using this as a crutch. She had sex. She's pregnant. Deal with it.

Amy told me she had wanted to do things in a certain order, preferably: (1.) be fifteen, (2.) go to high school, (3.) be in the band, (4.) meet someone, (5.) fall in love, (6.) get married, (7.) MAYBE have a baby. And here's the order in which Amy did do those things: (1.) fifteen/high school/band/ DEFINITELY have a baby, (2.) meet someone, (3.) fall in love, (4.) get married (to do).

Isn't there some saying if you want to make God laugh you tell him your plans? He must be laughing his head off right now. Amy's a regular walking sitcom, all right. She put a lot of thought into what she wanted and a baby wasn't even in her original top five. I asked why she had sex then. She said she didn't really think about it. That's what happens when you don't think about things. They come back in a big way to remind you that you should have.

Amy asked me to promise I wouldn't have sex until marriage. Honestly, sex is the last thing on my mind right now. It's caused some problems around here. First, with Amy's pregnancy and then with Dad cheating on Mom. I'm fine being the odd one out in this group. But just in case, I have condoms. I got them after Amy confirmed she was pregnant. I went to the grocery store when NedTed had his day off. I figured they must have a good selection if that's where Adrian buys hers. And they did, for a corner grocery store. Different colors and textures, even flavored ones. I just wanted a box with a picture of a baby and a big "X" through it. I didn't spend too much time picking which ones I wanted because I was afraid someone I knew would see me and it would get back to my parents, specifically my dad. So I grabbed the nearest box and got out of there. After paying, of course.

Amy told me she'd prefer I say no to sex altogether, but out of anyone in the whole world I would have thought Amy would have said no, and she didn't. Better safe than sorry, if you ask me.

The more we talked the angrier Amy seemed to get. I asked her why she was so angry. Even though she's fifteen and pregnant, things could be a lot worse. She's got a boyfriend who loves her and plans to help raise her baby even though it isn't even his. If anyone has a right to be angry, it's me. Everyone's moving out and even though Amy's pregnant, I still seem to be the one getting in trouble the most. How fair is that?!

She says she's angry at herself but I don't believe her. How can you be angry when you're too busy feeling sorry for yourself? There isn't enough room for both.

I wouldn't have had to go to the grocery store if condoms were given out at school! Just something to think about Principal Miller.

4:13 P.M.

Today took an interesting turn. Ricky, Amy's baby daddy, showed up. Thanks for joining the program that's already been live for SIX WEEKS!

Now that I've seen him up close I can see why she didn't say no. A picture's worth a thousand words, but in person, this guy's worth a bunch more. WOW. He's got a little bit of a *Rebel Without a Cause* thing going on. I get it. Ricky told Amy he just wanted to talk (like he probably did at camp) but I was sure glad those condoms were upstairs just in case.

Ricky had heard Amy was leaving town because he talked to our dad.

HE DID? WHEN?!

I can only imagine how that talk went. And Ricky doesn't come out alive in any of my scenarios. Yet here he is, standing in our living room. It's a real George Juergens miracle.

Later on, I asked Dad about his talk with Ricky and brought up my surprise that Ricky made it through alive. He

I also find it amusing Amy's worried I won't say no to something. Hasn't she learned after thirteen years it's rare when I say yes to anything? Will I please do a favor for someone? The answer is usually no. Would I like to help with this? Again, it's a no. Can I try to be more like Amy? Yes, I could try. But no, no I won't. The only time I answer yes to something is when I'm asked, "Did you really think you would get away with this?" Why YES, YES I did.

told me he had every intention of killing Ricky, but when he saw him standing there, he realized he was just a kid. Like Amy. And it's hard to kill a kid when he hasn't had a chance to grow up yet.

I didn't push the conversation any further because my dad could always go back and kill Ricky if he changed his mind. Still, I wondered where the confrontation took place. I know Dad didn't talk to Ricky at Amy's school because we would have heard about it. Yes, that was a shout-out to Lauren and Madison. If they didn't talk at Amy's school, then where would Dad have seen Ricky? Supposedly Ricky spends all his spare time at Adrian's house making good use of those condoms.

Anyway, Ricky said he wants to be involved in the baby's life because he is the dad. This will certainly be interesting now that Ben's in the picture. He said he was going to come back when either Mom or Dad was home (this guy has guts)— hopefully Dad, but it'll probably be Mom. Definitely not both.

6:59 P.M.

My mom came home and asked how I got home from school. I could tell she already knew. I still threw out words like "taxi," "bus," and "walking" to distract her. She didn't buy it. I couldn't believe she was interrogating me about skipping school when Amy's nearby, fifteen and pregnant.

The good news is, all Mom did was interrogate me. Before all this band camp gone bad business, I would have been grounded for sure. But now that Amy's pregnant, and as long as I don't get pregnant, my punishment for little things like catching a ride home from NedTed is pretty light. A stern talking-to? I feel like I'm bonding with Amy's baby already.

I told Mom EVERYONE at my school is talking about Amy's situation. The high school social circle and the middle school social circle have merged and now have the circumference of the earth. Which, in case anyone didn't know, is huge and why I can say that literally EVERYONE knows. And I'm not just talking about the kids. The cafeteria lady wouldn't even serve me lunch until I gave her the "dish," pun

No wonder you and my mother get along so well, Principal Miller. You're pretty much on the same page regarding clothes and discipline. You two could share your office... maybe get a partner's desk. My dad has a few nice ones in the furniture store. I know that kind of setup would help save a couple of hours in my day and you two wouldn't have to call each other all the time. Get back to me on this.

Hopefully she won't get mad when she finds out NedTed has been parking across the street so he can offer me a ride anywhere I want to go.

intended, on Amy and her situation. The crossing guard wouldn't let me cross the street until I promised to tell her as soon as I know whether it's a boy or a girl. And people who never even knew I had a sister are stopping me to ask all about her.

Dad came home and suddenly I forgot about everyone else except the three of us. I gave him a hug and then went up to my room so he and Mom could talk. Amy and Ricky were still talking, too. Then Ben came over and he and Amy talked. Talking is good when it doesn't involve whispering and rumors.

Talking is good when it results in my dad moving back home and Amy staying, too.

Sept. 27th

7:17 A.M.

Today Mimsy showed up, which was a big surprise. Not that I wasn't glad to see her—it's just that I thought Mom and Amy were going to go to Mimsy's house and Amy would stay there for a while. Honestly, I was relieved. Instead of subtracting people from this house we're adding them, and because it's my grandmother it feels like an added bonus. Grandparents usually side with the grandkids on things because they like to spoil us and that includes supporting us in matters of parental warfare—which may be why Mom didn't seem so happy. She's normally the one who organizes stuff like this and when anything goes wrong it causes her to jump off the deep end. So when Mimsy walked through the door my mother's demeanor pretty much said it all. And Mimsy causes her to teeter near the deep end anyway. So naturally I asked Mimsy if she would stay for a week, and she said she would!

Mimsy would hang out with us all the time when we were younger. We would stay up all night watching movies and talking. Then when Mom would pick us up the next day we would be too tired to do whatever she had planned. It was usually something boring anyway. And she would get so mad at Mimsy and ask her why she kept us up all night. Mimsy would just shrug and say, "Why wouldn't I make the most of the time I have with my granddaughters? They didn't come here to sleep, did they? They can do that at home with you."

I picked up a lot of my arguing-with-Mom techniques from Mimsy. She always says if you state the facts, Mom won't argue with you. And it's true. I used this approach once when I was little, after I got home from a visit with Mimsy. I wanted to eat a chocolate bar for a snack but Mom wanted me to have an apple. I refused, saying I have never had a bad candy bar but have had plenty of bad apples. Mom relented and let me have my chocolate. But not before saying, "All right. No bad apples for the bad apple." It was still worth it. Thanks, Mims. And you'll be glad to know I'm still working on the most effective part of arguing, which is disagreeing without being disagreeable.

Mom's relationship with Mimsy kind of reminds me of our relationship. Not that we don't get along, we do, but we don't

Sept. 28th

9:12 A.M.

Amy and I are going to see Dad tonight. I wish we were helping him move back home, but he's already living somewhere
else—like, permanently. Great. The patriarch of our dysfunctional family has moved and we have to go off-site to visit him.
Amy and I probably won't stay very long. Maybe Rod Serling
can have his own stool there, too, so he doesn't have to keep
carrying the one he has here back and forth. See? I'm capable
of thinking of others sometimes.

I thought Dad moving out would help Mom calm down
about things, but boy was I wrong. She's more on edge than
ever. I don't know why. She's the one who insisted he move out

see eye to eye on most things. I drive my mom crazy like
Mimsy drives her crazy. That's why Mom sometimes calls me
Little Mimsy.

I'm sure Mom's also nervous Mimsy's here because Dad
hasn't moved back in permanently yet and she doesn't want
Mimsy to notice. Mimsy loves Dad. Mom told me when they
got married Mimsy kept waving at him from the church
pew. You'd think since Mom and Mimsy don't agree on most
things Mom would have ended up with someone Mimsy didn't
like, so it's funny the complete opposite happened. I bet Mom's
worried Mimsy will take Dad's side over hers when she finds
out they are having marriage problems. Mimsy once joked
that if Mom and Dad ever broke up, she would want Dad in
the divorce. Mom had probably planned on spending the
whole car ride up thinking of ways to get Mimsy on her side.

I found a piece of paper crumpled up in the trashcan in
my mom's bedroom earlier (yes, I was spying). It was a list of
reasons she should or shouldn't stay with Dad. Her reasons
she shouldn't were: he cheated on me, he makes crude jokes,
he belittles me, and cheese nuffs. I have no idea what the
cheese nuffs are about but I could see her other points. She
had only two reasons listed under the "stay with Dad" column:
Amy and Ashley. So much for that. She better think fast now
that Mimsy's here.

Or not. Mom told her Dad was in North Carolina to buy
furniture. He does go there twice a year to buy inventory for
his store, but that's not for a few months, so he's obviously
not there now, but Mimsy bought it.

86

THE SECRET DIARY OF ASHLEY JUERGENS   83

Word is he's sleeping in his store. I tried explaining to people he's a devoted salesman who wants to show how comfortable his beds are, but I don't think they bought it.

I get called out all the time when I lie, so I was definitely tempted to do the same when Mom told Mimsy that stuff about North Carolina. I do want Dad home, though, and it would be nice to have someone else like Mimsy on my side. But I'll go along with Mom's lie. I just wish she would come up with better ones. My thought is if you're going to lie, LIE. Like, Dad went to China to research wood stains for some custom pieces he had made or he went antiquing in some old castle in England. Anything but North Carolina.

Mimsy wants Amy to keep the baby. She said adoption is not an option. I hadn't even thought about adoption. Amy just decided to have the baby and I hadn't really thought about what happens next. But Mimsy seems to have given it quite a bit of thought. She was telling Mom that Amy and Ben should get married (See? I told you grandparents always side with the grandkids!) and everyone will help out with the baby, including me. That's fine, I'll help out. Since Mimsy doesn't know Dad moved out, I'm assuming "everyone" also includes him. And then . . .

Well, Mimsy got confused between a crib and a kitchen drawer and things went downhill again. I should have known something was going on with her because the last time she visited she came into my room and called me "Anne," then asked why I had dyed my beautiful red hair black. I thought she was joking because Mom and I don't really look alike.

Mimsy always loved to point out how I was so much like and Amy was like Mom. When I told Mimsy my nam Ashley, she looked startled for a minute, then laughed said it's no fun getting old. It's true at her age and it's t mine.

She later admitted to us all that she forgot to take m tion for her Alzheimer's, which we didn't even know sh I offered to take care of everyone because, let's face it: just continue to get more complicated. Except with me. I told me to get through this stage of my life and then we'd talk about me taking care of everyone. What doesn't realize is I'm already on the next stage of my started taking care of Amy when I realized she was pre didn't I? Some nights I don't even finish my homewo I fall asleep before my head hits the pillow. Taking Amy does that to me. I even dream about Amy and wh I can do to help her and her baby.

I can see why Mimsy decided to move into an a living care facility. Life kind of wears you out.

and now she wants us to report back on all the details of each interaction. If she was so curious, she shouldn't have made him leave in the first place.

6:07 P.M.

We're here. Well, actually, Amy's out in the living room with Dad, Ben, and Ben's friend Henry, so I had to escape. I came here to visit Dad, not Amy's boyfriend and his friend. Thank goodness I brought this journal disguised as homework. The place isn't as bad as I thought, but something's not right. It seems like the displays my dad sets up at his furniture store. There are pictures of us, and stuff to sit on, but it doesn't feel like my dad's staying here. I asked if it's his girlfriend's apartment but he said no. Could have fooled me. There's so much perfume wafting around here I feel like I'm on the first floor of a department store.

Something else doesn't feel right. There's only one bed in the guest bedroom. This wouldn't seem odd except my dad *owns* a furniture store. A pair of twin beds is not hard to come by. So if Amy and I were to sleep over we'd have to share one bed. And since she's pregnant, technically I would be sharing a bed with two people. Wonderful.

7:13 P.M.

I started going through the room (which is fine, right? It is technically my room after all) and I found a drawer full of condoms. Dad skimped on an extra bed but made sure Amy and I had enough condoms to get through the year? No way, I don't believe it. Unless Amy's pregnancy scared him into submission and he'd rather be safe than a grandfather for a second time. Still, it doesn't make sense. I looked around for a hidden camera but didn't find one.

Gotta go, somebody's coming—

7:44 P.M.

That was weird. Ben's friend Henry brought me pizza. Which was fine except he didn't leave after he brought it, even after I told him to. He said he was tired of people telling him what to do and he wasn't going to leave because he's a MAN. Great, he brings me pizza plus all of his emotional baggage. His girl-friend sure did a number on him. So I let him stay and be a man in uncomfortable silence.

I like uncomfortable silences as much as the next person but usually people look around the room or at something else while they're being uncomfortable. Henry stared at me the whole time, so I had to put a stop to it. I said we could either talk or he could continue staring. He actually wanted to continue staring. Things must be really boring in the living room if he'd rather come in here and stare at me.

He asked if I'm allowed to date since I'm only thirteen. He was flirting with me. Wow, one of Amy's high school friends was trying to ask me out. A girl can't even get a slice of pizza from a guy without him wanting something in return. I was glad Dad was still out in the living room so he didn't hear any of this because he'd just start bragging about how right he is about guys. Then he'd throw Henry out.

You think I drive my parents crazy with what I DO say; you should see how they react when I don't say things. Case in point: Amy's pregnancy. Again, that's why my PROTEST AGAINST PARENTS was so successful. It was a silent one.

Maybe he asked me out because I'm Amy's sister. Maybe he figures since Amy gave it up then I might give it up, too. I told him since Amy's pregnant, I'm probably only allowed to breathe and that's it. I'll probably get sterilized before freshman year. He said that would be a shame because I'm really pretty. I might even be the most beautiful girl he's ever met, he said. I was tempted to tell Henry it's more flattering—and might have a better outcome, seduction-wise—to say, "You *ARE* the most beautiful girl I've ever met." But I didn't want to interrupt him. I have to admit, it was nice to hear. I can see why girls get sappy about that stuff. I can also see why Amy did what she did. Being told you're pretty leaves you open and vulnerable. And why wouldn't you be open if it meant you might get more compliments like that? I could tell Henry was in love with someone else and I was just a happy distraction, but it still made me feel good because he picked me as the distraction. How lame is that? I bet Ricky used that same line on Amy at band camp. If only Amy had realized she was merely a distraction. . . .

Also, with all the Amy stuff and my parents probably getting divorced, it was nice to have someone ignore all that and just see me sitting there. To know I was alive in this back room. I felt like I was being paid attention to for the first time in a while. So I was glad Henry didn't leave. Even if he did keep staring sort of creepily.

I almost forgot—I ended up crying AGAIN. Great. So I'm a crier now and a sucker for clichéd compliments *and* my dad gave me half a bed. At least Henry promised he wouldn't tell anyone about the crying.

8:27 P.M.

The night got worse after that. I should have never let my guard down with Henry, because when you let your guard down and bad stuff happens . . . well, it hurts a lot more.

Dad's been cheating all right. But not just with any woman. It's Adrian's mother (and if mother is anything like daughter we are in real trouble). So he's not only dating someone else, he's living with her family. He's replaced us with a newer model.

Amy figured it out when Ricky showed up to see Adrian. I should have known, a drawer full of condoms next to the bed—of course it was Adrian's room. How stupid does Dad think we are?

I wanted to ask him if Adrian's mom is a "nice" girl since that's what he says guys like. Mom's a nice girl, even if she does get on my nerves sometimes. He's such a hypocrite— and now he's a liar, too, for pretending he's living alone instead of with a new family. Like we never would have put two and two together.

You know what that means. What reason does he have to ever move back? I know my family is annoying and dysfunctional, but I'd like everyone to be annoying and dysfunctional under one roof. It's what makes us a family.

9:35 P.M.

Amy and I came home to discover Mom had had company of her own. Ben's dad, Leo, was over. It was nothing romantic, but still . . . it made me want to put a NO TRESPASSING sign on our front lawn. Leo came over to tell Mom he was okay with Amy and Ben dating. Wow, Ben's dad is okay with his son dating a girl who's pregnant with someone else's baby? He's really understanding. I wonder if he'd let me move into his mansion. I bet I could test his patience.

At least something good happened to someone tonight.

Mom started interrogating us about Dad's dating life. The last thing I wanted was to talk to Mom about it, but she wouldn't stop with the questions. I told her about Adrian's mother but Amy said Dad assured her they aren't dating anymore and he was just using her condo for our visit. It still doesn't excuse the fact he cheated on Mom with her, but I'll take it anyway. Maybe this will make Mom jealous enough to let Dad come back home. But I'm starting to have mixed feelings about that.

Honestly, at this point, I don't think I need to go to high school because my family is providing me with more drama than I can handle: dating other parents, jealousy, rumors. It's like some sort of horrible soap opera. Parents are always worried their kids will grow up too fast, but I feel like mine are forcing it to happen. And Amy's helping, too. I should just move into the garage and use the driveway as a hallway to the main house.

I brought up the "dating other parents" situation with Mom, and then Amy threw Henry in my face. She said I was doing the same thing by getting involved with Ben's friends. Henry brought me food. What was I supposed to do? I tried to get him to leave and he wouldn't. She should be getting mad at him, not me. I told her Alice broke up with Henry and they weren't going out anymore. I could tell Amy was upset that I had found out something about her friends before she did. At that moment, I felt like those loser gossipmongers Madison and Lauren, and that's not a good feeling. I'd rather be a crier.

So there we were. I was upset, Amy was upset, and Mom was upset. Then Amy said Dad was still living at the furniture store. So that rumor is true? How come Dad didn't tell me he was living in his store? He always tells me everything. We have an unspoken agreement that I am always the first one he tells things to. Amy said Dad told her while I was hanging out in the guest room. Mom was surprised he wasn't staying in a hotel or getting his own place. That means there really are money problems.

It made me think of all the times Amy and I used to have overnights at the furniture store. We'd play hide-and-seek and Amy would always hide in one of the armoires and I would hide in the same cedar chest because I hate playing hide-and-seek and since Amy would find me right away that meant the game was over quickly. It was fun then but I don't think it would be fun now. For one thing I wouldn't be caught dead sleeping in a display window. Does having no money mean I have to do that?

Being poor was going to make everything topple over. I lost it again. I begged Mom to let Dad move back home. I could talk circles around Amy's pregnancy and my parents separating . . . but I couldn't spin not having money. There is no way to talk yourself rich when the truth is you're poor. (I also don't think the fact that I'm reading *The Grapes of Wrath* for school is helping matters.)

Mom finally relented. She said he could move back if it was only for a little while, and until they could figure something else out. Having an opportunity at normalcy made me forget how mad I was at Dad. All I could think was that if Dad moved back for a little while, maybe it would become a longer while.

10:29 P.M.

Of course, I forgot my cell phone at Dad's Condo of Shame. I didn't mind going back because it meant I could tell my dad the good news in person. But I did mind when I walked in and saw him hugging Adrian. He was giving her something I had needed all day, let alone since I found out Amy was pregnant. This really drove the point home that not only was Dad cheating on Mom, he was cheating on me and Amy. Doesn't he know his daughters need him now more than ever? Adrian doesn't need any comfort. She gets comforted all day by LOTS of guys, especially Ricky. She doesn't need a hug from my dad. She can find her own father for that, wherever he is.

I could barely look at Dad, let alone speak to him. So I told Adrian to tell him he could move back in.

This whole time I've been trying to get Dad to move back home and convince Amy to stay. And now I'm the one who wants to leave.

Sept. 30th

8:07 A.M.

Okay, Principal Miller. You weren't lying to me. You do read this journal. I can tell because when I went to your office and picked it up yesterday you gave me a look you've never given me before. It wasn't pity (and thank you for that). Maybe understanding? Yeah, I think you understand a little bit about where I'm coming from now. I guess it doesn't hurt that my journal is also one-stop shopping for all your Amy gossip needs. I noticed you didn't say a word about the tight shirt I was wearing that came dangerously close to revealing my belly button as I reached out to take back my journal. I'm finding more and more that this journal does have its benefits.

So let's continue with the life and times of Ashley Juergens, shall we?

Last night, Amy asked me to help her decide whether to go to slut school or her old school. Mom wants her to go to slut school but Dad thinks she's better off at her old school.

I don't understand why this is even being discussed. She's still Amy, that hasn't changed. Why should she transfer just because she's pregnant? Now is when she needs us the most. It doesn't make sense to send someone away when they really need you. Especially to a place nicknamed slut school. I wonder what their school sweatshirt looks like.

"Slut school" is kind of a misleading term if you think about it. I know it's what everyone calls the school for young, pregnant mothers—but it makes it sound like you go there to learn how to be a slut. And if that were the case, I don't think Mom or Dad would want Amy to go there. If that were the case I think Adrian would be their valedictorian.

Anyway, Amy and I decided on a list to make things easier. Here's what we came up with:

SLUT SCHOOL +
Meet other young mothers
Avoid humiliation

SLUT SCHOOL –
Won't know anyone
Could fall behind
New school = new problems

<u>OLD SCHOOL</u> +
Friends
BEN
Band
Still live at home

<u>OLD SCHOOL</u> −
Ricky
Old school = old problems
People will avoid her
Still live at home

It felt like we were writing stuff down to waste time instead of making an actual decision. I think Amy is really worried people at her old high school will start avoiding her when it becomes obvious she's pregnant. I think her friends will surprise her. Except Lauren.

Since Mom was out of town helping Mimsy make her connecting flight to Europe, this morning should have been a nice start to a great day, with my dad being home and everything. Except I still wasn't talking to him. This is a rare occurrence and is always the result of something serious. In the past it's been for not taking my side in arguments with Mom, tricking me into going to a classmate's birthday party, taking the Classic Movie Channel off our cable package, and reselling my favorite chest of drawers at the furniture store.

So I communicated with Dad through Amy. I know she hates that, but I hate keeping secrets, so now we're even. I told him (through Amy) that I was on a hunger strike until Mom comes home. This was a lie. I was starving.

Dad told Amy he thinks she should go to school with Ben and her friends. Amy's still unsure. If I were still speaking with him I would tell him I agree. How can he know the right thing for Amy to do but fail so hard when making his own decisions? He's lucky I wasn't speaking to him.

9:32 P.M.

My hunger strike didn't last very long. I ate at school, since Dad wasn't around and he wouldn't know, then when I got home he heated up a lasagna Mom had made . . . and it smelled so good my stomach wouldn't let me be on strike anymore. It didn't taste as good as it smelled, though. Dads just can't heat up food the way moms can. It made me miss Mom a little. Not that I'd tell her or anything.

I really hate when she and Dad pretend to get along on the phone. Sometimes I'm offended by how stupid they think I am. Dad told Mom over the phone, "I love you, too, honey." Come on. I don't need to hear the conversation to figure out how it's going. I've been around long enough for that at least. I'd much rather have them here with their problems laid out on the table . . . after we had eaten all of the properly reheated lasagna, of course.

My dad and I called a truce, so I decided to talk about his

other daughter, Adrian. He said I was overreacting and to please stop calling her his other daughter. I told him he really hurt my feelings and he apologized. I told him he's not allowed to have other daughters besides me and Amy. He said he doesn't want other daughters, especially Adrian—she's a handful. She needed advice and he was the only one around to give it. I said I understood but next time I'd go looking for another father. My dad said I'd never find another father like him. I couldn't disagree there.

It's so much easier when Dad and I are working together and right now there's too much going on not to talk. Dad felt bad about not making Amy go to slut school like Mom wanted. I told him he should feel sorry for Ben, who got beat up at school for defending Amy and her slut school. I could tell Dad liked that. I think fathers like knowing if they aren't around to protect their daughters, someone else is.

Poor Ben. Even though he just scored a point with my dad, ever since he got involved with Amy all he has to show for it is a baby that's not his and a black eye. And he still loves her. His driver was right about him.

Dad used this opportunity to find out more about Henry. I told him Henry's on the rebound. I think my dad already figured that out or else he wouldn't have let us hang out alone in the back bedroom of Adrian's mom's condo with a drawer full of condoms. He also thinks Henry's a geek who wouldn't try to have sex with me. NedTed's a geek, too, and he's always trying to have sex with me, so there goes that theory. I didn't tell my dad Henry thinks I might be the most beautiful woman he's ever seen because Dad thinks if a guy says "hello" to me he's trying to get laid, so that piece of information might send him over the edge.

I told Dad I'm smarter than Amy when it comes to guys. He said he knows I have condoms. (WHAAAAAAAT?!) Like I said, I'm not Amy. If Amy had had condoms that night in band camp, we would probably be back to arguing about my wardrobe on a daily basis. But that's taken a backseat. (Except with you, Principal Miller ☺)

He confirmed Amy told him about the condoms. Great. I keep Amy's pregnancy a secret and she returns the favor by telling Dad about my condom stash. Nice to know there's a mutual trust between sisters in this house. I actually bought the condoms as an act of responsibility, not because of any intention to have sex. It's like when you buy a first aid kit. You don't intend to get hurt, but if you do, you're prepared. And even though Amy sold me out yet again, she can have some of my condoms if she ever needs them.

Amy and I used to trust each other with our secrets all the time. Sure, that was when we were really little, and even though the secrets were small . . . they seemed really big at the time. Like when I used to go to the movies with Amy and her friends. They'd see whatever chick flick was playing while I snuck into whatever rated R movie was playing. I always thought the movie ratings system was ridiculous. If anything's going to give me nightmares it's the chick flick. Who actually believes in Happily Ever After anyway? If they kept the movie going after the supposed happy ending then the horror genre would have a whole new subculture.

I was actually allowed to watch rated R movies when I was pretty young. But I could watch them only if I sat and listened along to my dad's commentary so he knew I wasn't getting the wrong message. Like when he let me watch *Pretty Woman*. He paused it every five minutes so he could tell me, "You know, this stuff doesn't happen when you're a hooker. It's RARE. Rare as in only in this movie rare." So I would sneak into the theater to watch R rated movies just for the peace and quiet. The blood, gore, and sex were just an added bonus. But I digress.

I've told this journal my closest secrets and deepest thoughts, but this journal really is just me talking to myself. And you, Principal Miller. Did you ever think we'd get to know each other so well? I would like to take this moment to remind you that telling anyone the contents of this journal would violate the principal/student code of ethics and you'd be terminated immediately.

Amy's secrets weren't as bad as mine, but that doesn't mean I've told anyone about them: (1.) she joined band to get close to a boy, (2.) the boy was not Ricky, (3.) she really likes Madison better than Lauren.

Anyway, even if I had told Amy's secrets no one would have really cared. But that's not the point. The point is I kept them because they were important to Amy. And she should be keeping mine for the same reason. But nothing's sacred anymore. Just because silly secrets have given way to pregnancy and condoms doesn't mean they are any less important.

My condoms really freaked Dad out. He told me I'm not allowed to have sex until I've moved out and am living on my own. I love when parents tell us to follow a rule they haven't even followed. Who was it that was living in this house, married to my mom, while having sex with another woman?

Ding! Ding! Ding! If you said George Juergens, you are correct!

Some may defend him by saying he was learning through his mistakes, but I call it hypocrisy. Deep down Dad knows he was wrong. He says he hates himself sometimes. I told him I hate him sometimes, too, but mostly I love him. I'm not ready to tell him how much because I'm still mad at him, but it's a lot. I'm hoping even though Mom probably hates Dad a lot right now there's still a little part that loves him, too.

Oct. 1st

11:00 P.M.

Amy ended up back at her old school. She was wrong about people avoiding her, even Lauren. So I updated our list:

OLD SCHOOL +
Friends, even Lauren, will support you
BEN
Band
*Still live at home**

   *Hopefully both Mom and Dad will continue to join us.

Oct. 4th

Once someone comes back into this house, it's become a rule of thumb that someone else must leave. Mom went out of town, and then Dad came back. Now Mom's back and Amy's gone. Well, not really gone, just at Ben's all the time. I can understand. He lives in a huge house filled with sausage servants. I bet Richie Rich lives in his very own wing, just like Steve Martin's mansion in *The Jerk*, only instead of a water cooler with red and white wine it has diet and regular soda. It must be nice.

You'd think they'd invite me over once in a while. I have been a good friend to both of them in this crazy situation and a dip in an Olympic-size swimming pool sounds nice right about now. Maybe they're worried I'd cramp their style as boyfriend/girlfriend, but in a house that big would they even know I was there? I wonder if Ben's ever gotten lost while walking around in his own house. I wish we had a big house like that. Then Dad wouldn't have to move out. He'd just choose another room and the problem would be resolved. Well, one problem out of many, anyway.

I'm surprised Mom and Dad are cool with Ben and Amy spending so much time together, but I guess they figure since she's already pregnant there's not a lot more that can happen. I asked Amy what she and Ben do when they're alone together and she said, "Talk." Like she doesn't do enough of that over here. She was getting on my nerves anyway. Still, I miss her, even with the constant pregnancy complaints and cravings. I walk past her room and it's weird how empty it is . . . and exposed.

That gives me an idea . . .

8:43 P.M.

Well, it took less than five minutes to find Amy's diary. And another thirty seconds to get the lock open. I didn't even bother looking for the key. At least it wasn't heart-shaped. She doesn't know about my journal (at least I don't think she does) but I've seen her write in her diary before, so I knew it existed. She thinks she's being so secretive but her nervous

I'm sorry for showing Dad your diary, Amy. But you did tell him about my condoms, which wasn't even necessary, since you know I'm not using them. And if you even know I showed Dad your diary then that means you found this journal, which I highly doubt. But if you did, then I'm going to give you a friendly, sisterly tip. Do not hide your diary underneath your pillow. It's unimaginative and easy to find and gives Mom a chance to catch up on your life during her laundry days. Also, when keeping a diary you should include actual, interesting stuff that's happening to you—like getting pregnant at band camp. Not fill it with a bunch of cheesy poems.

energy practically points a neon arrow to its hiding place.

I've never tried to find it before. Mostly because it's Amy's and I thought it wouldn't be very interesting. That was before band camp and Ricky and getting pregnant and Ben. Now I'm interested. And so was Dad when I showed it to him.

The poems in the diary were even more painful to read out loud. If I had known these were in here I wouldn't have bothered Dad in the first place. He kept thinking there were hidden messages about sex in every line. I wish. That would have made this diary a real find. If you don't believe me, here are some samples:

The start of my week,
Lying in my bed,
Staring at my feet,
With thoughts in my head

Really exciting stuff. You wouldn't know this is the same girl who went off to band camp and got knocked up. My dad's translation: "Who is she lying in bed with? I'll kill him!"

Trust me, it gets worse. And by worse, I mean even more boring:

Sitting on the couch,
Walking to my room,
Sitting at the table,
Searching for the moon

You would never know this girl has a boyfriend she supposedly is head over heels in love with. My dad's translation: "Who does she want to stare at the moon with? I'll kill him!"

Some of her poems were obviously written when she was having pregnancy cravings:

Cookies, cakes, brownies, and pies,
Pickles, pepperoni, olives, fries,
Milkshakes, sundaes, sandwiches, and steak,
I wonder which I can get my mom to make.

My dad's translation: "Why is she so hungry? Is it because of all the sex she's having? I'll kill him!"

I told Dad if these poems are related to her sex life, then Amy isn't having very good sex. Most likely these poems are a metaphor for no sex (Ben scored another point from my dad). The only thing they indicate is that Amy's in a new relationship and nothing's come along to spoil it yet. She needs heartache, yearning, and betrayal. Basically, a bad relationship makes a good poem. So in a way, this is good news.

Once the baby comes, I bet Ricky will prove quite inspiring.

Dad immediately forgot about the bad poetry and wanted to know how I know about good sex. Even if I didn't live down the hall from my pregnant sister, I still have access to a computer and the Internet. Nothing's really a mystery anymore. And if it is, I can solve it in about two seconds using Google. Some of those rated R movies filled in the blanks, but I wasn't about to tell him that.

He didn't seem to be listening because he started giving the sex talk. I had planned on this reading of Amy's diary as a fun father-daughter bonding experience. Now we were going down a road I definitely hadn't planned on taking. I was going to read another one of Amy's silly poems when he switched gears and told me about the day I was born. I was expecting a boring hospital story with an exaggerated number of hours in labor thrown in. Instead, Dad told me Mom went into labor and arrived at the hospital too early, so to kill time they took a drive up the coast. That turned into a police chase (that sometimes happens when you're going 90 mph and don't pull over), which became a police escort back to the hospital. I was close to being born in the backseat, but ended up being delivered in the hospital just in time. Dad never told me that story before. I didn't know my entrance into the world had been so exciting. Everything after it has been kind of boring up until now.

I wonder what Amy's delivery day will be like. I imagine she'll be at school walking down the hallway with Ben, complaining about her life as a soon-to-be teenage mother. By this point her baby will be so sick of her grumpiness he/she will try to escape, causing her water to break, which will flood the hallway and make everyone run for the nearest classroom. Ricky will be ordered to clean up the mess while Adrian pouts nearby because Amy's getting all the attention. Ben's driver will take Amy and Ben to the hospital, and Ricky will show up after he's sufficiently cleaned the hallway and students can safely walk to class. Then Ben and Ricky will argue about who gets to be in the delivery room until the doctor comes out and tells them the baby has already been born. Then Mom and Dad will see the baby and remember how happy they were when Amy and I were born, and they will agree Dad should move back in for good and we'll be a family again. Happily ever after, right?

Dad didn't have the same reaction about Amy's due date. He gets sad thinking about Amy's situation. When you're married and pregnant, having a baby is different. Everyone's excited and it's a special time in your life. Amy's only fifteen so things aren't exactly like that. Not everyone is happy because there's a lot of uncertainty: she's too young, the baby's dad isn't her boyfriend, and everyone's judging her.

But the one thing Amy does have is our support. Mom's, Dad's, and mine. And we're all going to figure out the best way to handle this together. So when Amy tells her baby what it was like when he or she was born, they'll hear a story like the one Dad told me . . . or hopefully like mine. A story where things started off kind of rocky . . . but it all ended up okay.

2:18 A.M.

I got up in the middle of the night to get a glass of water and saw a bag of perfectly good cheese nuffs had been thrown away in the trash. Dad also came in for a glass of water and saw me putting the cheese nuffs back in the cupboard. He told me to leave them in the trash. I asked why, since they hadn't gone bad. He said they are bad. Cheese nuffs ruin lives, ruin marriages. He gulped down the rest of the water in my glass, then walked back to his room. Um, what? If Mom and Dad are getting divorced on the grounds of cheese nuffs, I will be so mad at them. I remembered Mom had written down cheese nuffs on her list of reasons why she should leave Dad. Did he forget to write them down on the grocery list one too many times? Did he get cheese nuff crumbs in bed? Was Mom jealous Dad might love cheese nuffs more than her? I decided the reason didn't matter, only that there was a reason. I threw the cheese nuffs in the trash and went back to bed.

Oct. 10th

Every time I think life has calmed down for a second, a tornado moves in. And that tornado is usually Amy. Honestly, she used to be the most boring person. My parents would always ask, "Where's Amy?" and I would always have a boring answer. "Reading a book" or "practicing the French horn" or even "staring out the window." Now it's "she's pregnant" and "she's got a boyfriend but he's not the father of her baby" and today it's "she's marrying Ben." Okay, I didn't tell my parents that last part. How could I? I can still hardly believe it.

This morning I told her Dad was moving out and we needed to try to stop him. She acted like that was old news

111

and didn't seem concerned. I know it was understood Dad was going to be staying here only a little while, but I didn't expect it would really be the end of it. I thought he'd end up living back here for good. Amy said he's moving close by, but that's not the same as actually living here.

And how does Amy know where Dad's moving to? Why didn't he say anything to me? Dad and I are very close—we just bonded over Amy's cheesy poetry. Not that I could tell her, but we did.

I figured it must be because he knew how I would react and he'd rather Amy tell me. My reaction to things can be . . . explosive. But it's not my fault. I always give the appropriate reaction depending on whatever it is I'm being told.

I decided to use Amy and Dad's newfound closeness to my advantage. I told Amy she had to keep Dad from leaving. Maybe tell him she's having twins or something. She had to tell him not to leave, or better yet tell Mom that Dad can't leave. I worked hard to get him back here; now I needed Amy to help get him to stay.

But Amy wouldn't budge. She must have gotten up extra early today because she and Mom already got into a fight. Amy thought she could pass the baby off on Mom whenever she wanted, while she had a life. I rarely side with Mom, but this is definitely one of those times I do. How can Amy just dump all that responsibility on Mom? Especially now, when it looks like Mom has to find a job. And no offense to Mom, but maybe the baby should be adopted. It's not like Amy and I are doing so hot right now.

Amy DID NOT like the adoption idea at all. She said it's her baby and she doesn't want to give it away. Except to Mom.

It reminded me of when we used to babysit together. Five minutes after the parents left she'd hand me the baby and go watch TV. Then when the parents came back and asked about our evening Amy would say, "It went great!" and the baby was "such a good boy/girl." A baby's always great when you're not the one taking care of it. Maybe if Amy had performed her babysitting duties more thoroughly she would have been more careful about getting pregnant.

And Amy's dolls when she was little? She'd leave them out in the backyard all the time. They looked like they had been on a season of *Survivor*. I was about to mention this when she said she wasn't going to fight with me on her wedding day.

WEDDING DAY???!!!

And she wants me to be her witness. Well, yeah, I'm not going to miss this, that's for sure. Since the wedding's today, that must mean we're skipping the whole bridal shower, bachelorette party, and wedding-planning stuff. Fine by me! That stuff always seemed like stupid fluff that only leads up to the big fluff explosion . . . the wedding.

I don't know what good getting married does for Amy's whole baby situation. Let alone getting married without Mom and Dad's permission. Amy thinks marrying someone who will take care of her and the baby is a good thing. It is, but I think she should be more concerned about taking care of the baby herself. All this seems like a big distraction to overshadow the little distraction that's going to be coming very soon.

Amy said she was marrying Ben with or without me. Of course I want to be there. She said she wants to make her own decisions, and let's face it—the wrong decisions are more fun to witness.

2:13 P.M.

I got to see Amy's school today. Even empty it seemed better than my school—no offense, Principal Miller. It's bigger and I could tell no one gets bothered about what they wear. Amy told Mom she wanted to show me around, so she dropped us off while she got the car washed. We were really there to get fake IDs from some guy named Joe Hampton for the wedding, but I still looked around anyway.

I smiled nice and big for my ID picture because Amy said if I was her witness she'd tell me where Dad's moving.

I didn't want to tell Amy this, but that wasn't my first fake ID. This one is definitely an upgrade, though. I got a fake ID last year from another kid's older brother who sold them in the parking lot after school. It cost me twenty bucks and I got what I paid for. It was a used driver's license that had belonged to a woman with dark hair. It didn't even look like me, but after seeing his selection I didn't have the luxury of being picky. And it was the only California license he had, so I actually got the best one. I never even planned on using it. Like with the condons. It was just kind of . . . there. I eventually sold it for twice the price I paid because no one would ever believe it was mine

My big smile still looks like I'm bored, but trust me . . . I really wanted to know whatever she knew.

anyway. My dad would have been so proud. Of the profit I made on it, not because I resold a fake ID. But this Joe guy making the IDs at Amy's school had a nice operation going. It was definitely my picture. Only I lived in Nevada.

2:55 P.M.

Mom met us out in the hallway, which was a really close call. She and Amy talked about the whole job situation. Amy acted like she's been looking for jobs, but I know she hasn't. She's too busy planning a wedding and avoiding responsibility in general. Mom seems to be really looking, though. She told me she was surprised I didn't have anything to say on the subject. I know I tend to hurt her feelings a lot. I really don't mean to. It seems that way, but I don't. I've just been especially vocal lately because of Amy and Dad and everything. I'm afraid if I stop commenting on it I'll have time to look around and really see what's going on. It's a lot to take in. But I have to realize it's a lot for Mom, too, and my comments don't make it any easier. I'm really going to work on it and hope this journal helps. That's not to say I will stop making honest observations. Sometimes it feels like my family is stuck in some kind of Greek tragedy and I'm their one-woman chorus. A Greek tragedy always needs a chorus.

Then we got on the topic of Dad, which doesn't help when I'm trying not to make comments, because I don't want to think about him moving out. This is mouthy territory for me. So it was good when Ben and Henry walked up. Except when Ben introduced Henry to my mom as his BEST MAN. I felt like saying, "And you know Amy . . . the bride?" This wedding is going to be such a disaster. Everyone laughed it off, but I could tell Mom didn't get the joke. Thank God.

Then Henry decided to stop staring at me and ask me out on a double date with Amy and Ben in front of my mom. Mom thought that's what everyone was acting nervous about. Unbelievable. It's not a date, it's a way to get me to Amy and Ben's wedding without her getting suspicious. And Henry will probably use me to make his ex-girlfriend jealous. Now I'm a witness to their deceptive wedding and Henry's amorous entanglements. How romantic. Good thing Amy and I are sisters and friends or I would never have agreed to this.

After that was settled, my mom told me I could talk to her about anything—like double dates. She always gets like this with me and boys and dates. Even when I was little and went to Cotillion. At a certain point in the night it would be girl's choice and whoever I chose to dance with always turned into someone I wanted to date. She would ask me a million questions: Why did I pick him? Did I think he was cute? Was I hoping to go out with him after Cotillion ended? I didn't even want to go to Cotillion, why would I want to date someone from Cotillion? They made me choose someone. I would have preferred to stay in my seat during girl's choice. But Mom told me not to get kicked out because she couldn't get her deposit back. So I picked the guy who was closest to me and breathing. That was the extent of my thought process.

I wish I could tell her I had something much more interesting than a double date to tell her about. But I made another promise to Amy. Besides, I wanted to know where Dad was moving.

3:41 P.M.

I almost let the wedding secret slip out a few times before we got home. It was a little out of my hands. Signs from above— literally. On the way home we passed a church, a bakery, and a wedding dress shop. If "Going to the Chapel" had come on the radio, I would have confessed for sure. But I just sulked in my seat, wondering where Dad was moving since Amy still hadn't told me, even though she promised. I'm starting to think maybe Amy isn't a good friend. Or her brain is too preoccupied with wedding stuff to think of anything else.

We pulled into the driveway and I was kind of annoyed at how excited Mom was about starting her new life without Dad. At least I was until she opened the garage door and there he was, lounging on a recent couch sale item and watching TV.

HE MOVED INTO THE GARAGE!

This is great! He can give Mom her space but still be around for us. I mentioned before how I wanted to move into the garage. I can't believe I didn't think of this before. My dad's a genius. Birds of a feather flock to the garage, I guess. I wish I could say Mom was as happy as I was. She didn't like Dad taking over the garage as his proverbial doghouse. Amy had to reach over and physically remove the keys from the ignition so Mom wouldn't park the car on top of Dad and his new digs.

Dad used to set up our camping tent in the backyard when he and Mom needed a break. He would call it a "marriage vacation." Unfortunately, the tent was blown away one windy morning while Dad was inside brushing his teeth. I'm sure if the tent was still around Mom would have returned home and been unpleasantly surprised the next time she walked out in the backyard to do her gardening.

My dad took a break from watching TV so he and Mom could fight in the kitchen. I was actually glad they were fighting because it was a lot easier for us to get ready and leave for the wedding unnoticed. I'm not one hundred percent positive what the fight was about, but I did hear the words "money," "garage," and "urinal."

6:02 P.M.

When we arrived at the church, I was a little surprised. Particularly because I didn't see any church. I thought we pulled over because we ran out of gas or something. I never even knew this chapel was here. You know what? I don't think I wanted to know. I kept looking at Amy to see if she was getting cold feet, but she didn't look nervous at all. She was actually really calm, the calmest I've ever seen her. So was Ben. On the car ride over they kept looking at each other and smiling. Ben's driver kept smiling at me in the rearview mirror, as if to say, "I told you so." Henry kept smiling at me, too. I smiled at no one.

Albertson's Wedding Chapel is something to behold. I was pretty disappointed. Ben is the son of the Sausage King so I thought he would at least try to step it up a little bit. I know that making a commitment to someone else is supposed to be the only thing that matters, but this place looked like a cheap knockoff of the lowest-priced drive-through chapel in Vegas, except there was no Elvis to officiate. Elvis would have been an upgrade. It looked like one of Amy's original diary poems exploded in here. Henry told me the place wasn't as beautiful as I was and well, I should hope so. Even on my worst day I would hope so.

The "minister," or Albert as he's known here at Albertson's, thought I was Amy at first. Since I must have looked pregnant to him, passing for eighteen wasn't a problem. I still couldn't believe how far we were getting using these fake IDs.

Amy and I looked at each other and smiled before she walked down the aisle with Ben. I remembered when Amy used to fantasize about her dream wedding: her and Brad Pitt getting married on the beach in Hawaii. Ben's no Brad Pitt in the looks department, but he seems like a good guy. He's treated Amy well so far. And I have to say even though we were in a chapel that looked like it was decorated by the love child of Tacky and Kitsch, Amy seemed very happy and the moment was genuinely touching. So touching and lovely I didn't want to tell her there was no way this wedding was legal, since all of us are under eighteen, fake IDs or not.

Amy was surprised as she walked down the aisle to see a bunch of her friends had shown up uninvited. Lauren and Madison came in bridesmaid dresses, even though Amy didn't ask them to be bridesmaids. Typical. Adrian was there wearing something that shouldn't ever be worn in a church, so it's a good thing Albertson's is only a fake chapel. Henry's ex-girlfriend Alice came with Grace's ex Jack, Grace came with Ricky, and Grace's brother Tom came with his date, Tammy. Word must have gotten out around school about the wedding. This means Mom and Dad will be finding out about this very soon. That'll be exciting.

I know a lot of girls my age dream about their wedding day. I can't say the same for me. You might think it's because of Amy and the whole pregnancy thing. It's not. My parents' impending divorce might have something to do with it, but I think the real reason is I'm just not a romantic person. There is nothing scarier than that walk down the aisle, when everyone is looking at you and smiling. I *It won't be Madison and Lauren, Amy.* don't know what my dream wedding would be like because I'm not sure I'll ever want to get married. I think it's strange to dream about a wedding day. Shouldn't you be dreaming about the life you have after your wedding? It's not about the party, it's about who is still there to help you clean up after the party's over.

But Amy is getting married at Albertson's, and while it's very funny and sweet, it's not the wedding Amy deserves. That's why I'm glad it's not legal. Hopefully Amy can have the kind of wedding she's always wanted, someday when things aren't so complicated.

8:27 P.M.

These people I'm going to high school with next year can't dance. I could break out a couple of my Cotillion dances, but the only one I really remember is the Mexican hat dance. So unless someone throws a hat onto the center of the dance floor, I'm not going near there.

Here are some of the heinous moves I witnessed at Amy and Ben's wedding reception:

- The Sprinkler: perpetrated by the groom, Ben. He tried to act like he was doing it as a joke but I don't think you can be that good at "the sprinkler" without practicing at home.

- Raise the Roof: this was Jack's go-to move. The only problem was nobody reciprocated and he was raising that roof all by himself.
- The Running Man: Tom liked to do this one. Tammy liked to do this move as well, so I guess for her it would technically be called the Running Woman. They make a cute couple. I like her attitude.
- The Cabbage Patch: Oh, Henry. Poor Henry. Putting this visual in Alice's head is not going to win her back.

I can forgive the poor dance moves, since they did show up to support Amy and Ben. I just hope they get some practice in by the time Amy and Ben get married for real. I think I'm also getting a preview of what prom will be like and I am not pleased.

Instead of dancing, I hung out by the food table. Surprisingly, the Sausage King's son didn't really bring it, food-wise. A big disappointment. Other than that the reception was actually kind of fun . . . from a people-watching perspective. I thought Henry would come over to talk to me, but he didn't. He was too busy watching Alice dancing with Jack or trying to cut in on Alice dancing with Jack. Looks like the girl who might be the prettiest girl got dethroned. It's fine. I'll recover.

Most eyes were on Adrian. Just like they were when I went to the football game and she was standing out with the other majorettes on the field. At first I thought Adrian just likes attention from boys, but now I know it's because she's competing with Amy. Adrian's jealous of Amy. And the funny thing is Amy has no idea there's a competition, she's just a girl who got stuck in this situation and Adrian's a girl who wants to be in her situation. Adrian wants to be with Ricky and have his baby, but Ricky brought Grace to the wedding and he's tied to Amy for the foreseeable future. And it's driving Adrian insane. She can't even spell YMCA right now because she's so distracted.

I ran into Adrian in the bathroom. I didn't mention her obvious jealousy toward Amy. I did mention her trying to take my dad. She said she wasn't. I said in that case she must make it a habit to hug dads, and she was quiet. I told her he's got enough going on without taking on someone else's problems. Adrian said she knows and didn't mean to make me feel like she was taking my dad. She was trying to help him out that night by letting him use the condo and when he saw she needed help, he returned the favor by offering her advice and giving her a hug. She told me I was lucky, which I already knew, and then she apologized. I was expecting her to be more standoffish but she seemed to admire me for standing up for myself.

I thought I would go unnoticed by avoiding the dance floor, but people talked to me as they grabbed food so I got to know Amy's and Ben's friends a little better. Alice came over and asked if I was dating Henry. I told her we were just friends. She said, "Good. Not because I'm in love with him or anything, but because ninety-five percent of all rebound relationships end within the first month." I asked why and she said because that's when the other person realizes they can't move on yet. I asked if she and Jack were part of that lucky five percent and she said she didn't think so, but asked me not to tell Henry that. I told her not to worry. Henry doesn't need to date me to know he can't move on yet, either. Alice said, "Really?" I nodded and she smiled. Before she walked away she told me my chances of enjoying this party would increase fifty-seven percent if I attempted to dance. I told her I liked my odds where I stood.

Then Jack came over. You would think he hadn't eaten in a week. I asked him who the best kisser was: Grace, Adrian, or Alice? After almost choking on his food, he finally said Grace. And how did I know he had kissed all three of them? I said I saw him kiss Alice tonight, I know he dated Grace and besides, he can't stop staring at her, and as for Adrian, well . . . the odds were in my favor on that one. I suggested he lay off the onions if he was going to kiss anybody else tonight. He thanked me for the tip and left.

Grace came over to get some water and asked if I was having a good time and I said no. She asked why and I said because it's hard to let loose and dance when Amy's pregnant and so much is going on. She said she understood. Then we both looked at each other. I said let's just acknowledge the strange, gross elephant in the room: your mom used to be married to my dad. She said yeah, it is pretty weird. She still can't picture her mom with my dad. She can't picture anyone with my dad, no offense. I said none taken, but he does have his moments. Grace then said in some weird way we're almost like stepsisters. I said not really. She said but wouldn't it be nice to pretend, because then we could confide in each other and—I had to cut her off. I told her it was a nice gesture but I have my hands full with Amy. She said I seem like a very good sister. As she headed back to talk to Ricky I told her to be careful and use a condom. She said she didn't need a condom because she wasn't going to have sex. I'm sure Amy thought the same thing a few months ago.

Then Lauren and Madison came over, ugh. They wanted to reassure me there were no hard feelings even though I was chosen as the witness over them, Amy's best friends. I asked if they were jealous that Amy got married when they didn't even have boyfriends yet. Madison said she has a boyfriend, so that question was more for Lauren than for her. I said her boyfriend has been telling everyone at the reception he's with her only because he's a "lazy dater," so she might want to find someone else. They glared at me, and then walked away. I'm still mad at them for blabbing about Amy being pregnant. Although the fact that they showed up at all did surprise me.

Tom and Tammy came over to rest and asked if I would be their witness for their wedding, since I did such a good job at Amy and Ben's. I told them I was retiring, but why not ask Grace? They said Grace doesn't support their decision to get married so they have to find someone else. I told them they might want their families to be at their wedding. I have a feeling Amy will regret not telling Mom and Dad. I know Ben wanted his father here. Tom and Tammy said they couldn't tell their families because they would probably try to stop them from getting married. Then they left to go find alternate witnesses, while I wondered what was taking Dad so long.

Ricky wandered over to the table and we looked at each other. It was awkward. Neither of us spoke because, well, where do we begin? Good thing we didn't have to say anything because that's when Dad and Leo, Ben's dad, came barging in. I had bet money we wouldn't make it to the reception, so Dad must be losing his touch. Nothing breaks up a party faster than two old people who weren't invited. They marched us all the way down to the lobby. Ben and Amy didn't even get to say good-bye.

Dad dragged us back home to his garage pad and began lecturing us on the obvious: fake IDs are illegal and Amy and Ben's marriage isn't legal. Duh. Amy tried to argue the marriage vows they exchanged were real, but I guess that doesn't carry a lot of weight with someone who's getting divorced. She did go down fighting, though.

I expected Dad to tell Mom, but he said he had enough problems and didn't need one more. Great—ANOTHER SE-CRET! Those always end so well.

By this point I was so tired I just wanted to go to bed, but of course Mom was up and wanted to talk. Mom does this a lot now that we're getting older. She usually tries to ply us with food and have girl talk. I always cave because I'm hungry and I don't usually have a lot to say anyway. But this time I had already eaten *and* I had a lot of information I didn't want to risk spilling. At least Amy was there to share my discomfort. Mom wanted to make pancakes and hear all about our double date. Fine, besides the fact that my date and the best man tried to get another girl's attention all night long. I should have saved us all a bunch of trouble and just answered, "You mean wedding." When she asked whose, I would have said "Amy's." Then my next words would have been "good night" and Amy would've had to clean up her own mess.

But I didn't. I had to lie, lie, and lie. I find that when you're trying to cover up something with a lie and someone starts asking questions, it's best to be bare-bones literal.

How did tonight go?

"Fine."

Which it did until Dad and Leo came. I know Mom was talking about me and Henry, but we didn't really interact much. Once his ex-girlfriend Alice showed up with Jack, he couldn't be bothered with anything else. I wanted to tell Henry to grow a backbone, but that would have taken away from Amy and Ben's sweet-yet-not-legally-binding moment. After paying me a compliment he could have easily given the shrub outside, I told Henry I wanted the freedom to see other people. But back to Mom's girl talk:

What's Ben's house like?

"Big."

Yes, I've never been there. But it's the Sausage King's house and a driver takes him to school every day. I'm gonna go with big.

How big?

"Bigger than ours and a whole lot bigger than Dad's."

I figured since Dad is living in the garage this was a safe assumption.

Amy and I made a quick exit to our rooms. I was able to escape after three painful questions. And honestly, I felt bad for Mom. She seemed really excited about my (non) date, so you can imagine how she'll react when she finds out she missed Amy's wedding. That's supposed to be a big emotional bonding time for a mother and daughter. And even though it turned out not to be legal and Amy will probably have another one someday, there will always be this first one Mom missed because we lied to her about it.

I told Amy I was mad at her. She doesn't seem concerned that everything's building on top of everything else and once the baby gets here, we'll look back on these days as the easy ones. She doesn't fully realize it yet, but these commitments she's making right now are lifelong ones.

12:38 A.M.

I thought this entry was done for today but I was wrong. I think my parents are having sex in the garage. Yeah, I'm pretty sure that's what I'm hearing. Dad can install a urinal in there but he can't soundproof the place? I wonder if this means they'll get back together. I wonder if Amy's hearing any of this. It's so weird that Amy's the one who got married tonight but my parents are having the honeymoon. Why does this family do everything out of order?

All right, I'm going to bury my head under every pillow I can get my hands on and try to go back to sleep.

Oct. 11th

7:17 A.M.

I did not want to be around my parents this morning, especially knowing what I know. THAT THING WHICH I WILL NOT SAY OUT LOUD. But I had to go into the kitchen. That's where the food is.

I thought maybe it wouldn't be so bad because they'd probably be in good moods, right? I mean, they were both in good moods last night.

WRONG.

They were arguing. I offered to walk the five miles to school but they wouldn't let me. Mom really wanted to take Amy and me to school so she could try to get more information about our "date." Ugh, secrets are so much work, plus I didn't get that much sleep because of . . . well, you know, so my brain wasn't functioning at one hundred percent.

But Mom switched gears and asked the new Mrs. Boykewich about the job situation.

THANK YOU!

Amy mentioned she and Ben were going to try to find something after school. Since there was a wedding last night, everything Amy now says is accompanied by "and Ben." Mom seemed satisfied and went into the other room. I thought everything had gone well, but Amy panicked and suggested we just tell her. Excuse me? I'll let the one who actually got married tell her about the wedding. Just because I was a witness doesn't mean I have to tell people what I saw. Well, actually it does, but since the wedding wasn't even legal all my responsibilities as a witness are now null and void. I never saw anything because nothing even happened . . . at least according to the state. Besides, Dad didn't say we HAD to tell her. As long as we are obeying at least one parent, then we're being pretty decent kids.

11:02 P.M.

Amy came into my room tonight. Mom knows about the wedding. She ran into Marshall Bowman and he told her everything. Then Mom found the lovebirds at Ben's BIG house.

(See, I wasn't lying about that.) She wasn't mad she missed Amy and Ben's wedding, she was mad Amy still doesn't have a plan for her and the baby. And a wedding doesn't count as a plan. Yes! Mom and I agree on something else! Rod Serling just came in with something to say:

> *"Envision if you will a mother and a daughter on opposite ends of the bonding spectrum. When one goes up, the other goes down. If not for blood they would be strangers, passing each other on the street without so much as a glance. But they come together to talk some sense into Amy, finally meeting in the middle . . . in the Twilight Zone."*

I didn't tell Amy I agreed with Mom because I didn't want her to get distracted from Mom's message. And trust me, if I told her Mom and I agreed on something, Amy would've gotten defensive and all the good points Mom made would've been lost.

Amy stayed awhile and talked to me about it. Mom seemed to get through to her tonight. Amy said Mom talked a lot about responsibility and how it's not something you get with a marriage certificate. It's something you take. And Amy needs to start taking responsibility for things now.

I think the baby liked what Mom said, too, because he/she's been moving like crazy. Amy let me feel her stomach. She had a big smile on her face when the baby moved. I didn't want to gross her out, but the first thing that came into my mind was that part in *Alien* when the alien bursts out of that guy's stomach. Good thing Amy's baby isn't being born like that, although I think the pain level might be the same. I need to stop watching movies late at night. Unless Mom and Dad have sex in the garage again. Then I'm turning up the volume to eleven.

Oct. 15th

8:01 P.M.

Mom did eventually talk to me about my role in Wedding-gate. She cornered me in the bathroom the other morning. I swear, I'm either waiting to get into the bathroom while Amy's in there (she cuts in front of me now and says "I'm pregnant" if I start to get upset) or someone barges in while I'm using it. It's a lose/lose situation. But that's the Juergens family MO these days.

Mom told me I might think I'm helping by not telling her about things like the baby and the wedding, but I'm only making things harder for everyone, especially Amy. She needs to know what's going on so she can help. So if anything else should come up (and right here she took a deep breath), then I need to tell her right away. I just nodded and said okay, but I'm not sure if I meant it. And for the record, I didn't think I was helping everyone by keeping things from Mom. I'm as overwhelmed by this as everyone else. The reason I didn't say anything was simple.

I didn't know what else to do.

Oct. 20th

9:17 P.M.

We were visited by Reverend Stone tonight. His son, Jack, goes to school with Amy, so of course he knows about the whole pregnancy thing. I remember Jack from Amy and Ben's wedding reception. Not only because of his many sad attempts to raise the roof, but because he came with Alice, and seemed to pay more attention to Grace, who went to the reception with Ricky. Is it any wonder I like doing things alone? Look at what happens when you get involved with people. Love triangles don't even exist anymore. Only love octagons. And don't even get me started on how all this affected the women's restroom the other night. Every time I had to pee there was some discussion going on between Grace and Adrian, Alice and herself, and Lauren and Madison. I can't comment on the men's restroom, but all the guys seemed like they spent a little too much time in there, too.

Reverend Stone also thought I was Amy. (Do I look pregnant or something? Why does everyone think I'm Amy?) At first I thought he was here to perform an actual legal wedding, but he only came by to introduce himself. I'm sure he's heard from, well, everyone that our family needs help. He wanted to come in and talk, but Dad brushed him off. Mom took his card, but I'm not sure if it was to be polite or not.

I'm usually wary of people who make a living commenting on other people's lives from the outside.

I know you are amused by that last sentence, Principal Miller, so let me clear something up. Even though I openly comment on other people's lives, I don't make money off my comments. My insights are free and invaluable. And even though Reverend Stone doesn't technically get a salary, he receives donations through the church, which is the same thing.

I did make an exception in this case. Our family is at threat level red. I caught up with him outside and invited him to talk in Dad's garage living room. I was still skeptical. After all, I've been to his church. His sermons are okay, but it takes more than okay to keep my mind from drifting. I noticed during his sermon on sex before marriage that he kept looking at Jack and Grace. And that was only when Grace's parents (who always bookend the lovely couple when sitting in church) weren't looking at Jack and Grace. They can stare at them with those burning retinas all they want. Those two are totally going to do it before marriage.

I bet you're asking how come I didn't see the same thing happening with Amy. I wish I could tell you. I blame it on the moon and the tides and the position of band camp in regard to our planetary alignment. That kind of stuff causes people to act in a way they normally wouldn't. They should switch camp activities to nighttime and have everyone sleep during the day. That way if anything does go on, at least they'll have enough light to see it and stop it before it goes too far.

I was wrong about Reverend Stone not living life. He's lived it, all right. He used to be a drug abuser and lost a son. He's also been divorced, so he could definitely help Mom and Dad out in that area. He told me he likes how I question everything. Mom and Dad hate it. Again, another thing he could help Mom and Dad with. He's also seen the movie *Life of Brian*. That really surprised me, especially since it led to his calling to become a reverend. I've seen it, too, but it didn't change my life. I just thought it was really funny.

It's always weird to picture some people having a life before you met them or outside of how you know them. Like when you see a teacher shopping at the market. It's strange. You just know them from the classroom. You don't picture them ever going home or buying food. They disappear into the teacher's lounge after school and then reemerge sometime in the morning. I don't know where they go, but I never imagine it's to their homes. And I can't even imagine where you go, Principal Miller. It must be because we spend too much time chatting in that office of yours.

When I was six and Amy was eight our dad took us to the school carnival and he ran into a woman he knew who had a son about our age. They talked about boring stuff like the weather and his furniture business and then we pulled him away so we could ride the Ferris wheel. When she was gone we asked him who that woman was. He told us she was someone he "used to be engaged to." Amy and I couldn't believe there had been someone before Mom. This was before we even knew Dad had been married to Grace Bowman's mom before our mom. Why are men always so busy? We asked Dad what happened and he said it didn't work out, but kept stressing she was completely fine with it. If you're trying that hard to convince two kids you're right, well, I don't think you're so sure you're right. He doth protest too much.

Of course, when we got home we asked Mom for the real story. She told us it had happened when Dad was very young and he realized it was the wrong decision and called off the wedding at the last minute. And by last minute she meant they had already had the engagement party, had received most of the wedding gifts, and Dad's fiancée had bought her wedding dress. Dad tried to make it up to her by furnishing her new apartment after she moved out, but it took her a while to forgive him. He should have given her a better discount.

This made me think back to how he must have felt when he walked into Amy and Ben's reception. Obviously I know he wasn't happy at the time, but he must have felt sad that Amy had gotten "married" so young when he had almost done the same thing. Déjà vu through your daughter must be really strange. No wonder he didn't want to tell Mom about it.

My point is parents are included with reverends and teachers in the whole "you can't picture them having a life before you knew them" category. And if you try to bring it up and ask questions, they'll probably just tell you their life actually DID start when they had you. That's such an easy out. It usually means they had a wild time before you came along and don't want to tell you about it because they're worried you'll copy them. Try it. Trust me. Just go around them and ask another relative for the real story. My go-to is usually Mimsy.

Back to Reverend Stone. He hadn't come to talk about himself, even though that came up. He heard about Amy and Ben's fake wedding and came by to see if there was anything he could do. I brought up my parents' marriage because that felt like more of a crisis, since their marriage is actually legal. I told Reverend Stone I don't want my parents to get divorced and asked for his help. He mentioned doing his life's work and being sober was about as good as life could get, so I told him, "Great, then do your life's work and help me." I think Mom and Dad staying together would be as good as things could get for me right now.

He said Mom and Dad seemed unhappy. Gee, really? I bet he could hear them fighting and bickering from down the street. Couples aren't happy all the time, so it didn't make sense when he told me my parents are probably getting divorced so they'll be happier. I told him that wouldn't matter because then I wouldn't be happy. I know you think I'm self-ish for saying that, but I can't help it. All I've been doing these past few months is trying to help Amy and keep Mom and Dad happy so our family stays together. I want everything to work out the way I want it to for once. And I need help. After everything that's happened, is that so wrong?

Reverend Stone said he'd see what he could do. You don't hear that very much from people. Usually they just say they can't and leave. I liked Reverend Stone for that. Or Brian, as I secretly call him. But if he thinks I won't be sitting in church burning him with my own retinas until he saves my parents' marriage, then he's probably delusional enough to think Jack and Grace will wait until marriage to have sex.

After he left I stayed in the garage. Mom and Dad were still arguing about money and Dad's couch is comfortable. I had a pretty view of the neighborhood and it was nice and quiet. Until Amy came home. She asked what I was doing and I told her I was just hanging out. She decided to hang out with me and share her problems. If only Reverend Stone had stuck around, he would have gotten an earful. Being a good listener is his life's calling, not mine.

Amy earned $20 from babysitting, so I asked her how much it costs to have a baby. She threw out a vague answer of "thousands," so I did a little research later and broke it down:

Day Care: $650 a month
Preschool: $500 a month
Food: $200 a month

Clothing: $65 a month

Doctor: $100 a month[*]

*This is without insurance coverage

=$1,515.00 a month

Amy's babysitting money from tonight: $20.

Only $1,495.00 to go.

Whoops, I almost forgot about therapy for the baby, once he/she opens his/her eyes and realizes the insanity of it all: $750 a month.

So it's REALLY $2,245 a month.

And this is all calculated with a healthy baby in mind!

Wow. I can see why money causes problems. Mom still thinks Dad is hiding all of their money so she can't get any in the divorce. But why would Dad want to live in the garage if he didn't have to? It's nice hanging out in here once in a while, but I don't know about sleeping here. Just to be safe, after Dad left for work this morning I snuck into the garage and checked the couch and removed all the cushions. No hidden money.

Our talk about how much a baby costs was really getting to Amy because when you're pregnant, that's when you need money, but being pregnant makes it difficult for people to hire you and she really needs the insurance. Amy brought up starting her own business, but that won't get her insurance and you need money to start a business, and any money she gets now goes to the baby. Which leads me to ask what exactly is Amy qualified to do? Give French horn lessons, speak about abstinence, and babysit? As far as I know these jobs don't pay very much and don't come with health insurance.

I know she doesn't like talking about Ricky, but he is the father and the father shares in the financial responsibility. So I asked her how much Ricky is going to contribute. She hadn't really thought about it and of course had to call Ben to ask what he thought about it. It's kind of funny Amy thinks Ricky is stepping on Ben's toes in this situation. Ricky's the dad, not Ben. But Ben wants to be thought of as the father and doesn't want Amy to call Ricky about financially supporting the baby. So Amy hung up the phone with the same problem.

That's when I stepped in.

I volunteered to get a job. How hard can it be? You just show them you're not a complete idiot, start at the bottom, work your way up and then you get an assistant. Amy seemed skeptical and said it's not as easy as it looks. How would she know? She hasn't put much effort into job hunting and besides . . . I'm not pregnant.

I had a lemonade stand last summer. My neighbor Steven tried to compete with me by opening another one up across the street and charging less. Partners in the Protest Against Parents, enemies in business. So what did I do? I stayed open twenty-four hours a day and made sure each glass of lemonade was top quality—thanks to NedTed I got only the best lemons. I sent out an e-mail announcing all proceeds were going to the AJLS Fund. I still can't believe no one figured out it stood for Ashley Juergens's Lemonade Stand. I also spread a rumor about Steven's lemon supplier (I said his lemons weren't real lemons but a lemon and lime hybrid, and therefore his lemonade could be classified as limeade) and got a nice write-up in the Better Business Bureau. To top things off, I also had a tip jar. Steven was forced to shut down a week later. I closed my operation not long after his. I like going out on top and besides, my mom wasn't happy with my hours. Instead of his morning coffee, I would hand my dad his morning lemonade when he walked down the driveway to get the paper. My point is I have drive—enough drive to find a job.

At this time in the night I was getting tired of garage living. And there was a creepy guy parked across the street (not NedTed), who seemed to think we were having an unsuccessful nighttime garage sale. Must be because my dad still hasn't removed the sale tags from the furniture.

Amy wanted to go in right away. The stranger saw us looking at him and got out of his car. I'm used to the neighbors staring, but I don't like when strangers stare.

One time when I was little, I was playing in the front yard and a guy pulled up and asked if I wanted to get in his car and go somewhere. I told him I'd have to ask my parents first, and ran inside and did just that. Needless to say by the time my parents came outside he was gone. When you're older and that happens it's called getting asked out. And parents still get upset about it.

Turns out the stranger was Ricky's dad, Bob, who freaked Amy out even more, but I don't know why. I've never seen her so scared. She lowered the garage door and we ran inside.

Mom and Dad went outside and talked to him. He'd heard about Amy's situation and wanted to help pay, since Ricky's the father. Dad immediately took a liking to him. Ricky's dad also said Ricky likes to tell lies about him, but it's only to cover up Ricky's mistakes. He gave Dad his information and left. Amy told our parents Ricky's dad sexually abused him when he was younger. Dad seemed unsure Ricky was telling the truth, but Mom didn't think a child could lie about something like that. She threw the "adoption" word out again and Amy jumped on board right away. My dad (wait for it) didn't agree. He wants his grandchild around and in our lives. I know I've joked before about adoption, but I don't want the baby adopted. As usual, I'm on Dad's side.

10:34 P.M.

Amy and I talked in her room later. She brought up adoption with Ricky and he's not crazy about it either. He thought Amy suggested it because she's afraid Ricky will be like his father. I can see Ricky's point. If someone assumed I took after my mom just because she's my mom, I would die of embarrassment. Or mail some of her hair to another genetics lab.

I told her to stop worrying about Ricky and Ben because I'm getting a job. Amy isn't buying it (even though she can't really afford to buy anything right now anyway, ha-ha), but it's what I'm going to do. The thought of getting out of this house sounds pretty great right now. I can't even hang out in the garage without some weirdo lurking across the street. Might as well be somewhere else and making money while I'm there.

Mom came in and I let her and Amy talk, since they're in the same boat. Not pregnancy- and divorce-wise, but life-changing-wise. I hope Mom doesn't push adoption with Amy anymore. I feel like we have all been through so much lately, including the baby. And the baby seems to be handling things just fine, almost like he/she's part of the family.

Nov. 2nd

8:15 A.M.

Nobody in this family thinks I have any friends. Even Amy. I mention I'm visiting a friend after school and it's all anyone can talk about at breakfast. I don't see what the big deal is. I could have friends if I wanted, I'm just picky.

I used to be friends with this girl (who shall remain nameless) in second grade. She was new to the school and assigned to sit next to me. We became good friends and pretty soon we were inseparable. Then one day, out of the blue, she fell in with a new group and didn't want anything to do with me. She told them all my secrets (I frequently sent my mom's hair to a genetics lab for testing and had a secret crush on Rod

Serling) and acted like I had BO whenever I was nearby. During our class picture we stood next to each other because of the height thing and right before the photographer took the picture I yanked her hair back. It's my favorite class picture.

After this experience I decided to keep people at arm's length. Your friends are a reflection of you. And with friends like Lauren and Madison, it wouldn't hurt Amy to be picky either.

If you must know, the friend I went to see after school was Reverend Stone. I wanted to see how stopping my parents' divorce was going and if he could add stopping Ricky's dad from coming near our family to his to-do list. And maybe NedTed if he has time. But I didn't want Mom and Dad to know where I'd been, so I said I was visiting a gender nonspecific friend. I made it sound like I was hanging out with a mannequin on the ninth floor of the department store after-hours. That's one of my favorite *Twilight Zone* episodes, by the way.

I made it over to Reverend Stone's church after school. It was a definite step up from Albertson's, but it could do with a few less paintings of Jesus. I know it's a church and everything, but everyone sees Jesus a different way, so why does he have to be a white male with blue eyes? And why must he look the same in every picture? There should be a bunch of blank canvases hanging around with an arrow pointing at the middle with the words INSERT YOUR JESUS HERE. That way it's up to you and your imagination and no one gets offended. For example, my Jesus would look like Winona Ryder circa *Heathers*.

Jack showed up, which isn't unusual since he's Reverend Stone's stepson. I should have asked him what it's like living next to a church. You must feel guilty every time you look out your window.

Jack told me he likes the Jesus paintings. Of course he does. All he needs is a long wig and white robes and it's him. That's not art appreciation, that's vanity. He said his dad was stuck in traffic and he could give me a ride home if I needed one, but I told him I'd stick around. I can visit my "friend" only so many times before my parents want to meet the gender nonspecific pronoun.

I told him Reverend Stone's helping me stop my parents from getting divorced and another thing that has suddenly become a top priority. He just stood there and wouldn't leave, a little like Henry except without the compliments. I told him I need to get rid of Ricky's dad before my dad does it himself, so if he can call in a personal favor to (INSERT YOUR JESUS HERE) then that would be great, because Ricky's dad just got out of prison and I'd like to keep my dad from going in.

Jack wondered what Ricky's dad had done to get sent to prison. Since we were within church walls I told him Ricky's dad had abused children. He wasn't sure if his dad could help but wished me luck.

A woman showed up wanting to talk to Reverend Stone, too. She looked at the Jesus painting and said it reminded her of her ex-husband. Yet another awkward moment that could have been avoided with my INSERT YOUR JESUS HERE paintings. I'll have to bring up that idea with Reverend Stone. Maybe we could start our own business and then I could make enough money for Amy to take care of her baby and for Mom and Dad to stop fighting. Problems solved, and I wouldn't have to find a job after all.

I was surprised this woman was here to see Reverend Stone. She looked like she could take care of herself. Then again, so can I and I'm here to see him, too. Technically, I'm here for the other people in my life. I can't do it all.

I told the woman Reverend Stone was stuck in traffic and she said that happens a lot with him. She told me her name was Veronica and she couldn't stick around because she's a cocktail waitress and needed to get to work. There're not enough tips and they're low on staff. Plus her Jesus ex-husband hasn't been paying her the almighty dollar in child support. I told her I'm looking for a job if they're hiring. She asked if I was twenty-one and according to Albertson's I'm close enough, so I said yes. But I warned her I lack people skills and affection for alcohol. She hired me on the spot. Why was Amy making such a big deal out of this job thing? I got the first job I applied for and all it took was a little lying and a painting of Jesus.

4:30 P.M.

Veronica gave me a ride to work. She was really stressed out. Between work and her child and trying to see Reverend

Stone, there wasn't enough time for things like eating and sleeping. I didn't want to bring up the fact that her car didn't sound so hot and the check-engine light was on. I think she needs a new fan belt. Her troubles made me think things weren't so bad at my house after all.

Veronica introduced me to everybody and got me set up with my uniform and locker in the back room, even though I didn't have much to put in it. The nickname for my waitressing section was Heartbreak Hotel, because everyone who sits there just got their heart broken and likes to face the door to check out all the singles who walk in.

I kept my cell phone in my pocket in case Mom and Dad noticed I was still at my "friend's" house and decided to check up on me. I got a text message from Jack saying he saw Ricky's dad buying drugs and the police arrested him. I got a job and helped get Ricky's dad arrested and out of our lives. Not bad for a first day's work. Everyone seems lazy next to me. Speaking of that . . .

The job wasn't hard at all. I wish I got more tips than compliments, but then again, it was my first day. I'd approach customers to take their orders, but they always asked, "And what's your name?" Since I'm not a people person I'd cut them off if they got too chatty, which meant they ordered sooner, which led to me turning over the tables quicker.

Some people would start to tell me how their boyfriend/ girlfriend dumped/cheated on them and how they were lonely/ sad/confused. So I would tell them about my fifteen-year-old sister who is pregnant and newly married to her boyfriend

I was worried he was here on a date, but he wasn't. He was meeting Leo for dinner. It's nice the in-laws get along, don'tcha think?

who isn't the father and how her baby daddy's father was just sent back to prison and my parents are getting divorced because my dad had an affair with my sister's baby daddy's girlfriend's mother. That always shut them up and they ordered more drinks in order to try to make sense out of what I just said. I was on a roll until I realized my next customer was my dad.

I ran away and crouched down behind the bar. Veronica came over to see if I was all right. I was doing fine until my dad leaned over the bar and saw me. What's he doing out of the garage anyway? I was having such a good first day of work!

He immediately dragged me to his table to talk, which wasn't going to help my turnover rate at all. I told him I was working to help Amy support the baby. He said it's Amy's job to support the baby and she feels the best way to do that is to give it up for adoption. I told Dad that was my point. I don't want Amy to give the baby up for adoption. I know my dad feels the same way about the situation, but it's not his baby either. He told me he knows where I'm coming from but my waitressing tips don't belong to me because I'm too young to work there and I should give my money to Veronica, which I did. When I was collecting my stuff from my locker, I told her she should use the money to get a new fan belt.

Then Dad called Mom to come pick me up, so I eaves-dropped while my dad and Leo talked about getting rid of Ricky's dad. I didn't want my dad to know I had been to see Reverend Stone earlier, so I couldn't say anything about Ricky's dad being arrested. Thankfully, Leo didn't think they should handle the Bob situation themselves. The Sausage King has a good head on his shoulders, just like Ben. He should hang out with my dad more often. Maybe stop by the garage some-time for a beer and to watch the game.

6:20 P.M.

Amy sent me and Dad a text message saying, "IT'S A BOY!" A nephew. I'm so relieved I don't have to refer to him as he/she/him/her anymore. I'm going to be an aunt to a little boy. I'm so glad it's a boy and not a girl. This family doesn't need any more girls; it's drowning in estrogen as it is.

Wait a minute. What am I talking about? This little boy will be going home with another family. A family that prob-ably won't have an awesome aunt like me or a mother like Amy or crazy grandparents like my mom and dad.

Why does it seem like all the happy news around here im-mediately turns sad?

I looked over at Veronica, who was busing tables and pick-ing up what little tips people left behind. Here's a woman who was making ends meet without the support of her baby's father, with a car that barely works, a reverend who keeps missing appointments, and a job that doesn't even provide a decent paycheck. All for her child.

Amy needs to stop thinking about "poor Amy."

Nov. 11th

5:36 P.M.

I walked into Amy's room looking for a fight. I admit it. Sometimes you need a good fight. With all the pressure building up inside me, I'd rather explode of my own free will than somewhere unexpected. Which can sometimes happen when you're at, say, church and the pastor gives a certain sermon on movies and the corruption of youth and it really rubs you the wrong way and you yell out "Liar!" Yeah, it happened. It wasn't Reverend Stone's church but it was one we used to go to until we were kicked out due to my vocal participation. My dad thought it was hilarious and yelled out, "Yeah, what she said!" but my mom and Amy were mortified.

So in order to save Amy from further mortification she was going to help me vent on my terms. At her. And I did have a reason to be angry with her.

But when I walked in and saw her reflection in the mirror, Amy disappeared and all I saw was a pregnant girl. Can I fight with a pregnant girl? Is that allowed? Lord knows that kid's going to need a little fight in him with the last name Juergens, but I'm not sure he should learn to fight in the womb. But that doubt all changed as soon as I saw the pregnant girl trying on clothes. It confirmed what I suspected, so I called her out on her behavior. Because the pregnant girl was, after all, still Amy.

I asked if she was interested in Ricky. Ricky's supposed to come over tonight to talk and Amy seemed to be taking a long time picking out what she was going to wear. A little too long.

I must have walked by her room five times and seen five different outfits: peasant blouse, sweater, and jeans; blue dress, scarf, and tights; short-sleeve shirt over a long-sleeve shirt and jeans; long sleeve shirt, vest, shorts, and tights and oversized sweater and jeans.

It's pretty much your dream closet Principal Miller.

And when I came in she had on yet another outfit. Amy's done this type of thing before. If she's going somewhere and knows a boy she likes is going to be there, she spends a long time trying on clothes in front of the mirror. She was like this when packing for band camp and when she first started dating Ben, and she hasn't moved away from that mirror since she found out Ricky's coming over. That's my case, Your Honor, the prosecution rests. A slam dunk if you ask me, but no one ever does.

She told me she's not interested in Ricky, she has to meet with him so he can agree to the adoption and then she can start interviewing couples.

I really hate this whole adoption thing. I don't want her to give my nephew away. What if he turns out to be the only normal one here besides me? We're just going to give him away instead of trying to balance out the crazy in this family? That makes no sense. We should all be giving this some serious thought. My dream is to someday have my own peanut gallery and he could be my #2. My nephew needs to stay in this house so he can take my side on things.

I asked what would happen if Ricky didn't agree to the adoption. Amy said life would be over and she'd embrace teen motherhood. Dramatics are definitely not lacking in this situation, so I told her to stop it. She's not the only pregnant teenager to ever exist.

I tried bringing up responsibility with her but it came out wrong. I mean, it came out right at the time, but looking back on it now it was the wrong thing to say. I said if she had been responsible six months ago—and then she didn't even let me finish. She pushed me down to the floor and pinned me.

This is what I wanted, right? To have it out? I admit she took me down a lot faster than I expected. I could have fought her off, but she's pregnant so it wasn't a fair fight. She just repeated that she's trying to do the right thing by meeting with

Ricky. I didn't want to tell her that repeating something doesn't automatically make it right. She already had me pinned. She let me up after I stopped struggling. I find when people overreact to something you've said that usually means you're right on some level.

I helped her up but stood my ground. I said she does need to meet with Ricky, but she doesn't need to meet with Ricky ALONE. I wanted her to admit she was a little interested in him, but she said she wasn't. I didn't think she was being honest with me and felt someone needed to stick up for Ben. Ben's a good guy and cares about Amy and the baby.

But Amy seemed ready to explode and I felt if I continued to ask her about Ricky it would have led to another takedown. The kitchen was safer. Mom and Dad were in there, but all they do is argue. They don't pin each other down . . . except when they're in the garage. . . . Why am I even going there?!

Mom was making appetizers in the kitchen for Amy and Ricky's adoption meeting. Why doesn't she throw in candles, a bottle of wine, and some music while she's at it? Is this a date or a discussion? I spotted stuffed mushrooms, which means Mom's really pulling out all the stops to get Ricky to agree to this adoption. She makes stuffed mushrooms only for faculty meetings when she's brought in to discuss something I did at school. I know you enjoy them, Principal Miller.

She said she was meeting with Reverend Stone about potential adoptive parents. Brian better help me tonight like he promised in the garage, otherwise I'll make sure his "Reverend" title is revoked.

Mom told me not to chaperone the evening, but that doesn't mean I won't be listening in anyway. I could listen near the kitchen so if anybody left the room suddenly I could run in there, or I could listen by the family room and run to my room if anybody came around the corner, or I could listen in the hallway between the living room and the kitchen and pretend I was just passing through if anyone saw me. I'm going to go with that last one.

I told Mom Amy might try to tackle Ricky like she did me. She could take him, too, trust me. Mom immediately asked what I had said to get tackled. She had the same reaction as when I yelled out during the sermon. It was all my fault and not the pastor's. People tend to forget ministers, pastors, and reverends aren't perfect. If they were, they'd be, well, Jesus. I know Reverend Stone would agree with me on this. That's why I like Brian.

I told Mom I was tackled because I don't approve of this adoption. And heaven help anyone who doesn't agree with someone else in this family. As usual, she sided with Amy and said I need to support her and her decisions. But I feel I should have a say when her decisions affect the whole family, including a member who's on his way and can't speak for himself.

There was a knock at the door but it was Ben, not Ricky. So there would be a chaperone after all. I bet he's afraid Amy's interested in Ricky, too. Poor guy. I hope he didn't bring his squeaky voice tonight.

Amy wasn't as happy to see Ben as I was. And when Ricky got there he immediately said he didn't want the baby to be adopted, so it looked like there might not be a meeting after all. Ricky didn't mind Ben staying, so Amy was outnumbered. I didn't feel like getting tackled again, so I took some of Mom's appetizers and hid in the hall by the stairs where I could still hear everyone. The apps were pretty good, I must admit. I didn't get a chance to try the stuffed mushrooms, though.

Amy told Ricky if he doesn't want the baby to be adopted, then he should take the baby. Then Amy can have a life and Ricky can have the baby.

Umm, excuse me? I don't want anyone but Amy to have the baby. I hope this is a negotiating tactic.

Ricky told her he didn't want to get a job and drop out of school. Amy asked Ricky what he is willing to do to raise their son. Ricky didn't say anything.

Wait, does he even know Amy's having a boy?

Wow, she hadn't told him yet. Ben knew but Ricky didn't. Ouch. That should make Ben feel pretty good, though.

Ricky said his son would be better off with two adults instead of the two of them, but he doesn't know how to fix the situation. Ben doesn't either. Amy just told them to talk it over and let her know what they decide. I'm liking the game Amy is playing here. It looks like besides a baby, she's finally growing a backbone.

That was close. Amy left the room and I had to run into the bathroom with the appetizer tray. I couldn't hear as well but was able to rest the tray more comfortably on my lap. It was a cold seat but still a seat.

It was pretty difficult to make out what Ricky and Ben were talking about. I decided I should find Amy and talk to her. I set down the tray of appetizers in the bathtub and found her in her room.

She seemed disappointed when she turned and saw me at the door and not Ben or Ricky. She asked what I wanted, and I told her I'd been listening to everything that was happening in the living room. She looked like she wanted to tackle me again, but I said I was listening because I care about what's going on and I know she does, too, and neither of us is happy with the way things are going right now. She said I was right but she didn't know what to do. That's why she left. I told her she must be kidding, because I don't know why anyone would let two guys make an important decision like that. Especially when one of them is Ricky. She smiled a little at that but didn't say anything.

I told her she needs to be the hub of this operation because, let's face it, she is already and without her leading it everything falls apart. She can't just walk away from things. Not with a baby. She knew I was right. Not because she told me, but because she got up and went back into the living room. I ran back into the bathroom and found a very cold appetizer tray. It didn't matter, because things had fallen apart in the living room.

Ben and Ricky hadn't come up with much. By the time Amy walked back in the room Ben was leaving and telling Amy the decision was really up to her and Ricky.

Wait, what? Ben was supposed to argue against adoption! Come back!

7:38 P.M.

I was in the kitchen when Mom got home. I gave her the update. Ricky and Amy fought, Ricky and Ben fought, and Ben and Amy fought. It's the same old song and dance except this time with appetizers. Nothing got solved because no one wants a baby and now Ben won't answer Amy's phone calls.

Then Mom accused me of telling her this so she and Dad would get back together and take care of Amy's baby. She suggested I meet with Reverend Stone a few more times in order to learn something.

Brian, you have failed me and ratted me out in the process. I wonder if she knows about all our meetings. Since I had missed him at his office the first time, I paid another visit to Reverend Stone the other day. I told my parents I was seeing a showing of *The Grapes of Wrath,* since I was reading it for school. In reality Reverend Stone and I were catching a screening of *Life of Brian*. Before the movie started I suggested that when he meets with Mom maybe he shouldn't be so enthusiastic about the adoptive couples he found. Hopefully then Mom would decide Amy should keep the baby and then she and Dad would decide to stay together. . . . I also mentioned my idea for INSERT YOUR JESUS HERE. Reverend Stone was intrigued and said he'd think about it. I'm having it copyrighted just in case.

Back to the broken record also known as my mother. She told me I need to accept the way things are around here: divorce, adoption, and me being too young to have a say in any of it. Only she has a say in what's best for me. And then I said something back to her. . . . I don't even remember what it was. I just said it to say it so she wouldn't have the last word. And unlike Amy or Ricky or Ben, I don't just leave in the middle of things. I like to stay and be the last one standing. Usually Mom runs off frustrated, like Amy, but this time she didn't move or look away. She had reached her breaking point and now it was all coming down on me.

She said I can't talk to her like that anymore. She knows I'm in pain but so is the whole family. She's sorry she can't make it better but that's the way things are. And the way I talk to her has to stop. I apologized, because deep down I know I deserved this speech. And she's right . . . I am hurting. I'm hurting because all this stuff is happening around me and no matter what I try or do or say, I can't fix any of it. Everything keeps moving forward and I say the things I say because I'm angry and want everything to stop. And I want to be heard. I just didn't know Mom was hearing something else this whole time. I always want a reaction but this isn't the response I wanted. I have to keep reminding myself that as much as I'm hurting, it's nothing compared to what Amy, Mom, and Dad are going through. Mom gave me a hug and I told her she's an idiot, but only because I was the one who felt like an idiot. Old habits are hard to break, okay?

From now on when I feel the need to say something that might hurt Mom's feelings, I'm going to bite my tongue and write it in my journal. Starting now:

Mom, if you had followed all of this advice you've been giving Amy about taking responsibility, maybe Dad wouldn't have cheated on you.

9:13 P.M.

I overheard Amy on the phone later with Ricky. She told him as far as their son goes, they are doing things her way. I was pretty impressed. It seems that besides a backbone she also grew a pair. But my admiration quickly subsided when I realized this meant Amy was going to give my nephew up for adoption. What would have made that speech even better is if Amy had told Mom she's doing things her way, which means she isn't giving my nephew up for adoption. I didn't have the right to be upset with her decision. She was just taking the advice I had given her earlier.

Nov. 20th

12 NOON

We were late for school this morning so I had to run up and get Amy. She said she wasn't feeling well because she's pregnant. I don't think she's feeling well because Ben still hasn't called. Or it could be she's made the decision to give her baby up for adoption and still has to tell Ben about it. Or it could really be because she's pregnant. Whatever it was it has put Amy in a bad mood. But I had something to snap her out of it.

During my brief stint as a cocktail waitress, I had done pretty well and made $100 in a couple of hours. But since I had broken the law (AGAIN), my dad made me give my hard-earned $100 to Veronica, the cocktail waitress who hired me.

She felt bad taking the money, so she gave me her ex-husband's ring. She seemed thrilled to get rid of it and told me she's finally ready to move on and giving the ring to me would be the final step toward closure. I'm always happy to help out in someone's recovery process, so I took it off her hands.

Veronica and I have kept in touch since I left my job and dare I say . . . become friends. But don't tell Mom, Dad, and Amy that. Since she's a single mother I've been asking her advice on behalf of Amy and what she thinks I should do as an aunt-to-be. I'm hoping that when Amy (hopefully) decides to keep the baby, I'll be ready. Veronica taught me how to put on diapers using an old Cabbage Patch Kid I had when I was younger. We practiced burping, bathing, and rocking the doll to sleep. Now that Amy is further along in her pregnancy, Mom and Dad don't notice when I sneak out of the house as much. Veronica gave me the ring the last time I visited, after she taught me how to make baby food from fresh fruits and vegetables.

But I didn't know what I was going to do with the ring until now. Poor Ben's a married man with nothing to show for it. I mean, he has Amy, but I think he would appreciate the gesture. Once he finally calls her back.

Amy still wasn't happy because what good is a wedding ring when your husband's not talking to you? That was exactly Veronica's predicament . . . and the whole child support thing. I didn't tell Amy this. I didn't want her to think I was giving her something cursed or a bad omen. I thought of it more as an object someone didn't get a lot of use out of but maybe Amy could.

Amy said Dad found a couple to adopt the baby. That was fast. Who does Dad know that wants to adopt a baby? And why is he helping with this? I thought he didn't want his grandchild to be adopted? Now all of a sudden he's sitting in his garage plotting an adoptive parental takeover?

Amy told me the couple is Donovan and Leon and it would be an open adoption. Donovan and Leon would be great parents. I think I actually asked Donovan to adopt me at one point when I was little, so I get why Dad thought they would be a good idea. Donovan is a good person to go to for advice. He's always encouraged me to be who I want to be. But in this case I want to be an aunt. If Amy and Mom aren't going to budge on the adoption thing, then having someone you know and trust adopt the baby would be the next best thing to keeping him.

But I don't think this is about trust, at least as far as Amy's concerned. It's about passing along the responsibility Amy should be taking. Amy likes doing this. She's constantly doing this. And now with something big like this baby, she's seeing it's not so easy to pass the responsibility on to someone else.

There are so many kids out there that need good parents (LIKE ME!) that giving my nephew away seems like kind of a waste. Amy's perfectly capable of taking care of this baby, and I think deep down she knows it, too.

And think of how much fun a nephew would be. Someone who can look up to me. Maybe he'd have Dad's humor and

Mom's stability and be musical like Amy and judgmental like me. How can we let another family enjoy a person like that? I know it's what Amy wants, but has she even thought about the person she might be giving away? Speaking of giving away . . .

Amy should be in a good mood now that she's found good parents to adopt her baby. But she's not because she's thinking of Ben. Ben isn't the person who should be on Amy's mind right now. The baby is, so I tried to get the ring back because Amy doesn't deserve it. But she wouldn't let go.

Stupid Ben. I'm so mad at myself for not seeing it sooner. And I'm mad at Amy for choosing Ben over her unborn son. I don't understand why love means having to give up something so important.

9:31 P.M.

It's not a good day to be living in this house. Everyone (but me) agrees on the adoption and Mom and Dad (not me) have come to a mutual understanding about the divorce. They were talking about getting on with their lives when I walked into the kitchen. You know what that means. It means the new life starts and the old life becomes irrelevant. Well, I'm part of the old life and think I'm very relevant. So to make my point I opened the refrigerator and threw an egg on the ground.

I know what you're thinking. What was that about? It must symbolize my broken family or Amy giving up her baby or my broken dreams. WRONG. The crazier things get around here the more dramatic you have to be to get your point across, and that usually involves props. The egg was the first thing I saw besides a watermelon when I opened the refrigerator door, and I didn't want to throw the watermelon because that would involve a lot of cleanup and the possibility for injuries.

11:59 P.M.

Later that night I went snooping in Mom's desk and found a list of everything she and Dad want to keep in the divorce. Mom wants the house, fully furnished; the car; and any money he's currently hiding. Dad wants his collection of funny salt and pepper shakers, the right to take any food he wants out of the kitchen before he moves, and the option of having me live with him if that's what I want. Unfortunately, Mom crossed that last one off. It made me feel good Dad remembered me, though. Must have been the egg smashing.

Nov. 30th

7:34 A.M.

Amy's still Ben-sick, which is worse than any type of morning sickness I've ever seen. I don't get how a guy can make you feel like that. I've had guys make me feel queasy because the stuff they say is so lame (Hi, Henry), but not sick to the point I'm wondering what they're doing every second of the day and why they haven't called me.

Dad didn't even know that Ben and Amy have been fighting for the past week. The garage isn't exactly a million miles away, and I know for a fact it's not soundproof (ick), so I don't know why he's acting like he's living under a rock. Of course, I'm sure being in a fight with Mom really weakens his awareness. Still, Amy never hides when she's upset about something. Which is probably why Ben isn't returning her phone calls.

Dad can't imagine what is making them fight, since Ben's been with Amy through this whole thing. I told him Ben thinks Amy might have feelings for Ricky. He didn't believe it, but Amy did have sex with Ricky. On the other hand, when you're pregnant your feelings and hormones are all over the place, so I wouldn't be surprised if Ricky got hit with some emotional shrapnel. This house is quite the war zone.

Dad wanted to "nip this in the bud" and went upstairs to talk to Amy. Brave man. I didn't want to tell him that bud's already in bloom. And once Amy and Ben break up, it's only a short breather until the next fight. And let me guess who will have caused it . . . the baby? Ricky?

I'm tired of my parents fighting or talking Amy down because she's fighting. I'm tired of being the messenger of everyone's fights. I think I'll find my own ride to school. If anything's worse than indoor fights it's fights in a car that last the five miles it takes to get to school. Why just fight in one place when you can take your fights mobile?

7:56 A.M.

I'm at the bus stop now. I'm a big fan of the bus stop. It's shady, there's a bench, and I'm not surrounded by people arguing. If it weren't for the morning traffic, it would almost be . . . peaceful. Someone's coming and he's trying to act cool. This should be annoying—

8:20 A.M.

I'm back. I wasn't thrilled when I saw who was approaching. It was a guy. I've had enough of guys complicating my sister's life, and I'm not really looking for a friend at the moment. Okay, I never am. But he ended up being kind of nice. He goes to my school. He transferred last year and seemed kind of hurt I didn't remember him. How can he expect me to remember him? He's wearing a leather jacket and sunglasses and trying to act cool. That's every kid at my school. And also Amy's pregnancy has been kind of distracting me lately. Of course, this *I blame you, Lauren and Madison!* guy Thomas already knew about Amy.

He told me his dog died. I felt sorry for him, so I let my defenses down. I can't compete with a dead pet. He offered me a cigarette. I wanted to ask him if his dog had died from secondhand smoke, but I realized it wasn't the right time (see, I'm getting better!).

I took the cigarette but not to smoke it. I was going to hold it and then throw it in the trash can as a dramatic gesture. I was thinking about this when Dad and Amy pulled up. Amy looked shocked and my dad looked upset (mobile fighting!). He asked if I was taking the bus (the bus stop must have blown my cover), then pulled away.

I know what you're thinking. I'm in trouble. But I'm not. My dad knows I don't like smoking. He's annoyed I left the house and that I'm holding a cigarette, but he knows Amy's more likely to get pregnant than I am to smoke. Thomas seemed to understand because he tossed the cigarettes. That's the only thing that bothers me about Rod Serling. I think the Twilight Zone should be a nonsmoking zone, too.

Thomas wanted me to skip school with him. Let's make it the next 4½ years and I'm in. With Amy knocked up I could probably get away with it, and he seemed nice enough, but I couldn't because I was waiting for Ben.

That's right. I called Ben. When your name's not Amy he picks up the phone right away. Ben's actually not a hard guy to talk to, so I don't understand how he and Amy got into a fight in the first place. Yes, I do—it's Amy. Like any guy, Ben needs to learn that even when he's not wrong, he still has to say he's sorry. He can be sorry he and Amy are fighting, and if Amy thinks he's accepting blame then who cares about the specifics. And I know Ben can do it. He apologized right away for being late. It slipped out no problem. He even offered to drop me off at school and have his driver write a note so I wouldn't get in trouble for being late. Ben's a giver.

I told him he needs to go over to our house and apologize

to Amy before she and Ricky sign the adoption papers. He said he couldn't do that. I think he feels partly to blame for the mess we're in. Not Amy getting pregnant (we all know who's responsible for that), but trying to be a part of something he's not. It's easier for two people to make a decision than three. And he is the ultimate third wheel in this situation. He told me he would rather put his feelings aside for the moment.

I found that to be very amusing. How can someone put their feelings aside when they were just put on full display at Albertson's Wedding Chapel?

Literally. The Juergens/Boykewick wedding photo is hanging in the hallway leading up to the chapel.

And do you know how I know they were on display? Because I WITNESSED it. Even though the state doesn't recognize it, I do. I have two eyes. I took part in the ceremony. And it wasn't Amy and Ricky up there holding hands and saying their vows, it was Amy and Ben. So for Ben to put his feelings aside for Amy and Ricky at this point is not an option. Not when he married my sister and threw a reception (with okay food and really bad dancing) to celebrate those feelings in the first place.

Ben countered with the whole "we changed our minds" argument. I told him Amy hasn't changed her mind about him. He may think Amy has feelings for Ricky (and let's face it, I did, too) but that's probably because everything would be easier if Amy did have feelings for Ricky. But Amy fell for Ben. And the truth is Ben is the best thing for Amy and the best thing for the baby. The two go hand in hand. I see it, why doesn't everyone else see it? I witnessed a lot more than their wedding at Albertson's. I witnessed the kind of person Ben is and the kind of person he is with Amy and the kind of person Amy is with him. He has earned a place in the baby's life and a say in the decisions made about it.

Ben didn't really comment on anything I said but I have a feeling he'll come around. At least, that's what I'm counting on.

Since the high school is closer to the bus stop, Ben's driver dropped him off first. I told him he was right about Ben being a good guy. He could tell I was still worried about Ben not talking to Amy, so he asked if I was in any hurry to get to school. I said I never was. So we got some coffee and talked. He told me about Ben's mother dying five years ago and how he's just starting to come to terms with it. Ben didn't have a choice whether his mom died or not, and he doesn't want to force Amy or her baby to make a choice between him and the rightful father, Ricky. He said one reason Ben might be pushing Amy away is because he's afraid she will eventually leave him for Ricky.

We went to the car wash and talked while the car got washed and waxed. He asked about that other guy I was talking to at the bus stop. I said his name is Thomas and I wasn't sure what I thought of him yet. He said looks can be deceiving, that I look intimidating but am easy to talk to. He told me to give Thomas a chance, and then he signed my late note for school. As I got out of the car he told me, "Ashley, you're doing just fine, in case anyone hasn't told you lately." I said thanks and hurried into school before I started tearing up. Again with the crying!

Later I got to thinking how I started this school year with no friends. Now I have three: Reverend Stone (aka Brian), Veronica, and now Ben's driver. I really should get that guy's name, since we're friends and all. And I have my nephew to thank for them.

Thomas, the guy from the bus stop, called me and we ended up talking all night. He admitted that he never takes the bus. He sat down at the bus stop only because he saw me sitting there. He usually walks alone to school. I wasn't sure if he was telling the truth or not. He really tries to act cool, even on the phone. I bet he wore his leather jacket and shades for the whole conversation. I hate when people try so hard, but I didn't tell Thomas because (and I would never admit this out loud) I like having a friend at school, even though I've never actually seen him around school. It still counts. And I like that he listens; I need someone to listen to me right now. And it was quiet tonight because I wasn't helping Amy or catching my parents up on her latest drama. I was just lying around and hearing a different point of view. Even if that point of view has to act like he's so suave. And as an added bonus, he doesn't make me queasy. But he doesn't make me Ben-sick either.

Speaking of illness, I couldn't really stomach listening in on the meeting between Amy and Ricky and Donovan and Leon. Don't get me wrong, I LOVE Donovan. Anyone who can put up with my dad for eight hours a day (at least) and keep an even temperament can certainly

Someone's not allowed to get mad at me for eavesdropping anymore.

take care of a baby. And Leon seems pretty cool, too. But it should be Ben and Amy meeting with them or, better yet, Ben and Amy deciding together they don't want to give my nephew up for adoption.

Before their meeting, I had a chance to catch up a little with Donovan. He took one look at me and knew I wasn't happy about this adoption thing. I told him he was right, but it was nothing personal. He understood but said me being unhappy about the adoption doesn't help his decision because I usually have good instincts. I told him he was right and then went to my room. But my curiosity got the better of me and eventually I walked into the kitchen and caught Mom listening in.

She was pretty upset. She felt Ricky was deliberately sabotaging the interview. In my brief time knowing Ricky, it seems he likes to sabotage his life in general. He's certainly done a number on this family. But in this case it's working for a good cause, so I say we give the guy a break. I'm just relieved Mom didn't overhear Donovan and me talking earlier.

When the meeting broke up, I was getting nervous that Ben wouldn't show. But when the doorbell rang, I knew it was him. Amy was angry Ben would rather show up and disrupt everything than return her calls. So he likes making dramatic gestures. Amy does, too. I should have tossed her an egg for added effect. But instead Mom, Dad, and I waited in the kitchen.

Ben gave Amy the biggest speech of his fifteen-year-old life. Ben's driver promised if Ben decided to finally come over and talk to Amy, he would go over with Ben what he should say on the ride over to make sure Ben had it down pat. And it showed. It was way better than anything he said at his Albertson's wedding. He loves Amy, he's a part of her life, he's a part of the baby's life, he'll take care of them, and he's the father—just not the biological one. He said he fell in love with her before he knew she was pregnant and nothing that's happened since has changed his feelings for her. IT WAS GREAT.

And Amy's reaction?

"I'll think about it."

Oh, Amy. If you only knew all the man hours I've put into making sure this moment took place. All you had to do was say yes. . . .

Dec. 2nd

7:53 A.M.

I headed straight for the bus stop today. I got up early, got dressed, skipped breakfast, and took my favorite seat on the bench. Thomas was already there waiting. He was surprised I got there so early, but I wasn't in the mood for another morning meltdown with the family. He wondered why my parents weren't more protective of their daughter taking the bus alone and I said it was simple: they didn't even know I left the house. He didn't buy it, which is understandable. If he had a fifteen-year-old pregnant sister he would know what it's like.

He took out his phone and said he was going to call my bluff. I told him to go ahead. He dialed my number and asked for me when Mom picked up. I heard Mom yell for me, then tell Thomas she'd give me the message. I was kind of hoping someone would notice I, the heart of the Juergens family, was gone and be ever so slightly concerned. But no.

Sometimes I hate being right.

Thomas asked if my invisibility was my fault or my family's. It's not my fault they don't notice I'm gone. They should be aware something's up because I LIVE IN THE HOUSE.

I do like the benefits invisibility gives me, though, like leaving when I want to and having the freedom to take the bus. It's nice. And . . . I do make the extra effort to be stealthy about it. But not being missed means that even when I'm there I'm not really noticed. Why doesn't my family notice I'm not there? Everyone knows I try to be vocal about things. Don't they miss that? Dad, are you around? He lives in the garage and I bet Mom and Amy would miss him if he was gone. This baby is slowly erasing my existence . . . just like the *Twilight Zone* episode where the guy wakes up and his whole family doesn't know who he is.

I avoided Thomas's question because there're two answers, and when there're two answers that usually means I'm partly to blame and no one likes to admit they're wrong, especially me.

I told Thomas my invisibility allowed me to get a job as a cocktail waitress and my age allowed me to get fired. Thomas asked how old I was and I realized even though we talk a lot on the phone, it's mostly been about Amy. He doesn't know anything personal about me. I'm invisible even over the phone. I told him I was seventeen. Hey, I've got a pretty good track record for lying about my age and getting away with it. He didn't believe me. I asked why I never see him at school and he said because he doesn't go there. He knew I went there because he saw me get off the bus in front of my school.

And then he stared at me like Henry, except it wasn't a "you might be the most beautiful girl in the world" stare. It was more of a "I like you, but I'm on to you" stare. And he didn't look away. He doesn't seem to be intimidated by me.

He admitted he's not in middle school. He's homeschooled, but his parents aren't very good teachers. Well, obviously, if they don't notice you're not in class at this very moment. He said he doesn't get along well with others. He's probably telling the truth, because only someone who doesn't get along with others would get along with me. He must have noticed my behavior on the bus. If someone creepy sits next to me or acts inappropriately, I don't mind telling them what I think in a very LOUD VOICE. People hate that. Isn't it weird that people who act inappropriately are the ones who hate being stared at the most? Then don't be weird! Like invading personal seat space and thinking I won't notice or say anything. Now nobody sits next to me on the bus . . . well, nobody except Thomas.

He asked if he could come over tonight. He said he's fifteen so my parents shouldn't freak out too much. I took his number because I wasn't sure I wanted him to come over.

I didn't tell Dad Amy never applied for that waitressing job. Besides, why would Amy even attempt waitressing after my amazing display of talent and $100 in tips after only a few hours? I could have been Amy's baby's sugar momma if Dad had let me keep that job.

With my family being the way it is, he might be the one freaking out. On second thought, I might as well bring him home. He could up my visibility factor.

I should have taken the bus home from school, too. My invisibility cloak stopped working when Dad picked me up and started interrogating me, trying to find out where Mom and Amy are working. So I'm on anyone's radar only when they need information? I didn't even know they had jobs. You miss one breakfast and you're completely out of the loop.

I called Amy to try to find out but she didn't want to talk about it and hung up on me.

Dad tried to think up places where Mom could possibly be working. He came up with: (1.) librarian in charge of the women's studies book section, (2.) salesperson at one of his competing furniture stores, and (3.) assistant to somebody lame. I came up with: (1.) clerk at adoption agency, (2.) band camp counselor, and (3.) started her own business called Mothers Against Their Teenage Daughters Having Sex.

For Amy, Dad guessed: (1.) twenty-four-hour babysitting service, (2.) working for Leo with something involving meat, and (3.) waitressing at that coffee shop she applied at before. For Amy, I said: (1.) professional whiner, (2.) certified procrastinator, and (3.) getting her BA in lazy.

I can't imagine Mom looking for a job with everything that's going on. But I know she's been on Amy to work, so it's great they found something. Especially since we have no money.

Dad laughed and told me we do have money to support the baby without Mom and Amy having to work. He doesn't want me telling either of them. Maybe he wants Amy to accept responsibility for her actions and Mom . . . Well, I think he's just having fun with Mom.

Since he was in such a good mood, I asked if I could have a friend over. He asked if this was an imaginary friend or the one with the dead dog. I said it was the one with the dead dog.

I'm the imaginary one around here. *Yes, that was a shameless attempt to gain sympathy, Principal Miller.*

6:01 P.M.

When Thomas came over, he seemed fascinated by Dad's garage-house-place thing. I wish my dad would close the garage door once in a while. He may not mind how he looks in his boxer shorts, but I know the neighbors do. With no soundproof walls, Amy being the talk of the town, and him sleeping in his store window before moving back here, I guess Dad doesn't care about privacy that much anymore. This garage setup must feel like a gated community to him.

Still, I have a visitor! Door down! I'd rather not answer any embarrassing questions if I don't have to. And Thomas totally saw the urinal. Great.

Thomas brought wine for my parents and when we sat on the couch he told me he hated small talk. It was kind of feeling like a date. I hope he knows I have no plans to get pregnant like Amy. I changed the subject to conspiracy theories, since I think life is one big conspiracy theory—manufactured by INSERT YOUR JESUS HERE. That was a joke I was going to tell Reverend Stone, but I changed my mind when he went back on his promise to stop my parents' divorce. He doesn't deserve to laugh.

Ben came to the door to drop off some ice cream for Amy to enjoy after work. Poor guy, Dad zeroed in on him right away. I knew he wasn't going to let Ben leave until he found out where Mom and Amy were working. It didn't take Ben long to let it slip out—the Hot Dog Hut. Wow, Amy's working at a meat place that isn't Boykewich's Butcher Shop? That's gotta hurt a little. Dad couldn't get to his camera fast enough. Before Thomas came over Dad joked he was going to get a picture of my first "friend" (little does he know I already have several), but it didn't take long for Dad to forget about us thirty seconds later. It's probably a good thing. Ben said Amy didn't want anyone to come down to where she worked, so she can't get mad at me for this one. Oh well, Dad will show me the pictures when he gets back.

The phone rang an hour later. Dad realized he had left me behind. AN HOUR LATER. This invisibility thing isn't getting better, it's getting worse. And hot dogs aren't going to make up for it. If he took decent pictures, that might help a little. We'll see. . . .

Thomas and I settled into a routine pretty quickly. The routine of a boring, old, married couple. I made him food and then we had a conversation that consisted of boring topics, almost as if we'd already run out of things to say. Just what I've always dreamed about. I don't think things are supposed to get that boring that quickly. And when it does, in my limited experience, it falls apart just as fast. He does spend his days getting homeschooled by his parents, so maybe this is normal for him. He didn't judge my dad's urinal, so maybe I should give him a second chance. Still, I liked it better when we hung out at the bus stop with the prospect of going somewhere. Now that we're at a destination, the excitement is gone. It might be a good idea to invite myself over to his house and check out his parents. I asked him how old he was. He finally admitted he's thirteen.

Maybe I should try to find an older guy, someone who's seen the world. Or at least the world outside the bus route. But I did learn something about myself. After hearing Thomas talk about his dead dog so much, I realized I wanted a dog.

Jan. 10th

It was opposite day today. My dad was in a great mood and Amy, for once, didn't want to be late for school. I almost started acting nice but thought it would be more fun to watch than actually participate. Then I found out why Dad was in such a good mood and mine went way downhill.

Dad has the picture he took of Mom at her new job holding a hot dog. He blew it up to poster size and hung it in the garage. He's trying to enjoy it as much as he can because Mom's not going to be working there very long. She met someone. An architect named David. She's interviewing for a job at his firm today and going on a date with him, which means fun time in the garage with Dad is over. Which is a good thing for my ears, but a bad thing for Dad. Seeing Mom work at the "weenie stand" yesterday softened the blow, but it's going to sink in soon that this new architect boyfriend of Mom's really means the end of their marriage. Mom moved from a hut to a high-rise pretty quickly. And Dad's still in the garage.

And Amy, well, she's started acting all motherly by telling me to eat right. She still hasn't decided whether she's going to give the baby up for adoption, but this maternal act tells me she's leaning toward keeping him. Dad and I decided to get Amy talking about the baby as much as possible, so she'll feel a tighter bond and decide to keep him. That's the plan anyway. You know how perfectly a Juergens' plan always goes!

I put the plan into action late last night. I collected every picture I could find of Amy holding a baby. Surprisingly, there were a lot. Amy holding babies at baby showers, family reunions, birthday parties. I also found a bunch of her holding me. Then I put them into an album and left it in her room. I snuck back in this morning and found it shoved into the back of her closet. That means she looked through it at least once.

I continued operation Mother/Son Bonding by talking about the baby the whole way to school. I wonder if he'll look more like you or Ricky? Maybe he won't look like either of you; maybe he'll look like Mom and Dad. He might even look a little like me (if he's lucky). Do you think he'll be good at sports or lean more toward music, like you, Amy? If he does, the tuba may be the more manly way to go, and it'll make him easier to see on the field. I wonder what foods he'll like or if he'll have any crazy allergies. Maybe he'll invent something that'll save the world, which would be good because we don't have any scientists in the family (if you trust science), or maybe he'll win the Nobel Peace Prize or be knighted or elected president.

I've never seen her so happy to see me off to school. I know I'm making things harder by talking about the baby, but let's face it, it is a hard decision. And it's one Amy has to make. And in order to make it she has to really think it all through.

Since I found out my only friend at school, Thomas, doesn't actually go to my school, life on the playground hasn't changed much. This is fine with me. I'm going to be surrounded by my sister's friends soon enough when I'm a freshman. I might as well enjoy the peace and quiet while it lasts.

I did end up inviting myself over to Thomas's house the other day after school. Not that it needs to be mentioned, but this was a huge step for me. My curiosity got the better of me, and I had to see his parents for myself.

They didn't disappoint. His mom, Carolynn, and dad, Jim, both work out of offices at their house. Jim's a lawyer who likes to scream on the phone a lot (even when he's not arguing) and Carolynn runs a housewife website that promotes her favorite recipes and products. She's always invited to promotional events by food companies and put up in fancy hotels, so she's not really home that much to homeschool Thomas. I didn't bring up the obvious fact that being away from home doesn't make you a very good housewife.

We also had the invisibility thing in common. But Thomas's invisibility wasn't his fault at all.

Thomas told me that's why he misses his dog so much. A pet is a good companion and provides distraction from your parents. His dog, Sammie, was a mutt and loved being outside, so Thomas walked him a lot. Going on walks by himself just isn't the same. I said he should get another dog and told him something I heard Mimsy tell a friend of hers once: "You can mark the different parts of your life with the different dogs you have had." She might have been referring to her past boyfriends, but since her friend had just lost her dog at the time, I'm pretty sure she meant actual dogs. Since Thomas still had Sammie's bed and toys lying around I knew he wasn't ready yet, but he said he'd think about it.

This made me think again how much I want a dog. Instead of remembering the days when Amy got pregnant and my parents weren't getting along, I would have fond memories of Chester, the golden retriever, or Nugget, the little teacup poodle.

When I got home, Amy wasn't there. I must have gone too far with all the baby talk. I called Dad to make sure he didn't forget to pick her up. He forgot. If she was in a good mood this morning, she's not now. And I certainly didn't help things. Dad asked if I knew where she was, but I didn't. Dad said he got sidetracked with his home loan and then hung up on me.

I just realized Thomas probably came over to my house because he was thirsting for normalcy and a boring routine. At my house?! Poor guy.

Home loan? Where is he moving to? Does Mom know? Does Amy? Where is Amy anyway? Dad lives here now, so he has to face me eventually.

Since I had the house to myself, I went looking through Amy's room again.

I want to make clear that I don't make it a habit of going through Amy's room. I started doing it only because of the pregnancy and I wanted to make sure she was telling me everything. And I want to see if there are any clues about which way she might be leaning on this adoption thing. Maybe I'm panicking over nothing.

I found her diary under the same pillow, but all that was in there were some more of those awful poems. I thought maybe she had another supersecret diary that had all the really good stuff in it, but all I found was a video in her jewelry box. I thought it was a taped high school band performance but it wasn't.

It was a video of Amy talking to her son and introducing Mom as his grandmother. I showed it to Dad when he came home—

Because I assumed he shot the footage and I wanted to know why I had been left out, but he didn't know anything about the tape. We figured it must have been Ben holding the camera. It was in the waiting room after Amy's doctor's appointment. It must have been shot right after Amy found out she was having a boy. Why weren't we asked to be in the video? Dad's her dad, and me . . . well, where do I begin? Let's start with all the secrets

At first I tried to get him to tell me about the home loan but he wouldn't budge. He kept saying not yet!

I've kept for Amy, starting with the pregnancy. How about all the support I've shown her and the temper tantrums I've lived through? I'm the aunt, don't I get an introduction? Since when did she feel the need to start leaving us out of stuff?

She did say in the video that "my dad loves you, my sister loves you. . . ." Thanks for the honorable mention but I would have liked to have told the baby I loved him on camera MYSELF.

To add more salt to the wound, the tape was made the day I started my waitressing job to help pay for the nephew Amy thinks doesn't need to see my face.

Dad and I felt shut out because the tape was obviously made for the adoption process, so my nephew will know where he came from. Have Mom and Amy really decided on adoption? I thought Amy was still thinking about things but this tape makes it seem like it's already a done deal. Is that why Dad and I weren't asked to be in it? Because we don't agree Amy's baby should be put up for adoption?

I thought feeling invisible was bad, but Amy just made me feel like I don't even exist.

I was really, really angry. Here I was watching Amy tell her son she's going to do anything she can to make sure he'll have everything he needs in life, and she's planning on taking away his family.

The baby's not going to see his mother in this video. He's going to see a teenager who went to prom and hung out with her friends and saw her boyfriend, while he was shipped off to another family because she didn't want to disrupt her dumb teenage life.

I imitated Amy's performance but Dad didn't join in and laugh like I thought he would. He said Amy's really struggling with things and it's not as if any of this is easy. Then Amy herself confirmed what Dad said—she was standing behind us the whole time. I was hurt by the tape and wanted to hurt her back so I'd feel better. She ran off, and of course I didn't feel any better. I felt worse.

Dad told me to talk to her. This house is one of the few places Amy can come and feel like no one's judging her and I've tainted that.

Dad and I went up to Amy's room. She felt ganged up on. Doesn't she know how Dad and I operate by now? There's no one we haven't mocked. No one's safe, especially not family. But she was hurt. I guess it's easier to go for the jugular when no one's in the room and you never see the damage.

I told Amy I know she cares about the baby. But that caring shouldn't stop after he's born. Just because you don't think you're capable of caring for a baby at fifteen doesn't mean you can't do it. I don't think she's even tried to think of herself as a real mother at fifteen. And why shouldn't she? There are so many people around who are willing to help and who think she can do it—her friends and us, her family. Keeping her son is the best way to show him she cares. And she can do it, I know she can. Just because some people think having a baby at fifteen is bad doesn't mean it has to be. And it doesn't mean you have to give up the things you love. You just have to find another way to do them. There's always another way. And that doesn't make them bad or worse than other ways. Things are bad right now, sure, but they don't have to be. Things are the way they are—it's how you handle them that determines the outcome. And I know Amy can handle this. I wouldn't be fighting so hard for her to keep the baby if I didn't.

Amy's been so busy telling herself the best thing would be to give the baby up for adoption that she's forgotten her other options. Dad told her she can keep the baby if she wants. I think Amy needed to hear that from him. And as soon as she realized maybe she could keep her son, everything opened up. Her friends offered to babysit, Grace found Amy a daycare job she can work at after school that will also take care of her baby during the day and provide insurance for them. . . . They made her see she's not alone.

Amy waited for Mom on the couch. Mom told her she could keep the baby if she wanted, but it's not going to be easy. Amy said she wants to keep the baby and knows she will be a great mom because she has such a great mom.

You've probably guessed by now Dad and I were eavesdropping. I told him Amy didn't mention us at all, we were left out again. But you know what? It didn't matter. All that matters is Amy is keeping the baby.

!!!!!

Feb. 4th

10:32 A.M.

I know most people like celebrating and throwing parties with gaudy decorations, but I find it to be overkill. You walk into a party store (not that I really do that often) and there's something for every event, well, every event except: Congrats! You got pregnant at fifteen the first time you had sex by a guy who isn't your current boyfriend! I wonder what kind of piñata they'd suggest for that. . . .

It should come as no surprise to anyone who's read my journal this far (Principal Miller) that my mom, in this case, is like most people. So she's pretty concerned about this baby shower Adrian's throwing for Amy and that it's done properly and that she's there to see all these special moments before the baby comes. I don't know why. It's just a big ploy to get in good with Ricky. I've got a tip for Adrian. Go to band camp. Apparently that's where all the action is!

A lot of people are skeptical of Adrian's motives, even Ricky. But some people defend her, like Grace, even though she's also been a victim of Adrian's where Ricky is concerned. I heard some people say Adrian was dating her stepbrother, so they don't think she's interested in Ricky anymore. Please. Even though she's related to her stepbrother only by marriage and barely knows the guy, she's using anyone she can who's around. She's obviously trying to make Ricky jealous.

Still, no one's called to invite my mom and she wants to go. I know this because she keeps asking me about it. It's always a bad sign when someone is asking me for party information.

I had no idea who was invited. I figured it was just Amy and her friends, since they were throwing the shower. Mom should just show up. No one else besides me and Henry were invited to Amy and Ben's wedding, but that didn't stop people from filling up the seats.

Mom ended up calling dad's ex-wife, Kathleen, to find out if she was invited and it turns out she was. So am I. Not only am I invited, I'm also being put to work. I have to write down every present Amy gets and who gave them to her. And I will do it with a smile because I'm Aunt Ashley and I played no small part in convincing Amy to keep the baby. I have to accept responsibility for everything that comes along with the territory. This includes parties and eventually . . . poop. Believe it or not, I can handle the poop better than these stupid parties. Thanks to Veronica.

I asked Amy what she wants for a shower gift. She said she doesn't have anything for the baby, only a pair of overalls. Shoot . . . that was the one thing I had written down. There are so many things to get a baby and a lot of them seem so ridiculous. (A baby-wipe warmer? Life is hard, baby wipes are cold. My nephew should learn this while he's young.) I hoped Amy would give me more direction. But then again, she doesn't have much direction herself at this point.

I decided to think on it a little more. I had other things on my mind besides the shower. Dad's moving out. Mom's excited about it and, believe it or not, so am I. I know what you're thinking. After successfully moving him back in (even though it was the garage) and trying to keep him here, how can I be excited he's moving? Easy. I'm moving with him. When he asked, I said yes immediately. Well, I said yes after he promised he'd get me my own bed so I don't have to share with Amy when she visits. I'm so relieved to be moving with him. It seems with the baby coming and Mom getting a job and a new boyfriend that this is the right thing to do.

Mom doesn't know yet, and as soon as she finds out I know her excitement's gonna give way to hurt. That's not what I want, but I also don't want to stay here without Dad. I don't know where we're moving but Dad said it's really close by, so we'll see Mom and Amy and the baby all the time. I know

Mom's going to see this as me leaving, but I'm not. I'm just taking an extended vacation from my current living situation.

Dad wants me to tell Mom. What a chicken. I know I'm a chicken, too, but he's an adult. I'm allowed to be a chicken until I'm eighteen, so he can be the one to tell Mom. He says she'll be upset at first and then it'll be okay, just like with the divorce. Again, since it'll be okay, he should tell her. Besides, I've got packing to do and all of his things are already boxed up in the garage.

3:00 P.M.

I almost told Mom I was moving a couple of times in the car on the way to Amy's baby shower. But then I thought if I tell her, she'll be sad, and then she won't enjoy the shower. And the shower's already going to be bad enough.

Mom almost didn't find the place. Identical condominiums were on both sides of the street and the numbers were all hidden by shrubs. Even though I had been there before to visit Dad, I was in no hurry to get there. I wouldn't say I had the fondest memories of the place. I changed my mind when driving around got old and finally pointed out the lonely blue balloon tied to a sprinkler head on the sidewalk. Balloons are always the indicator of a nearby party. I was tempted to not say anything, but I was already dressed up and holding a gift-wrapped box containing a days-of-the-week bib set. So let's do this and get it over with.

It seemed like I wasn't the only one who was less than thrilled to be there. Tammy, Grace's brother's girlfriend, didn't want to come either, but when you're a girl it's just something you have to put up with sometimes. Grace's mom's car was hit in the parking lot, so Tammy was telling me about that. Great, I missed the one exciting thing that's going to happen today.

We got to Adrian's condo and Amy wasn't there yet. Ben was going to drop her off so she and Ben must still be looking for the blue balloon. Besides this and picking me up at the bus stop, he's usually very punctual.

It seemed like Grace was hosting the shower more than Adrian. I never even saw Adrian. But I know she lives there. We shared a bedroom for a couple of hours.

The longer we sat there the more I kept thinking, the later Amy arrives, the later this thing starts, and the longer we have to stay. It's always awkward when the guest of honor hasn't shown up yet.

One year my mom threw my dad a surprise birthday party at the furniture store and he showed up three hours late. It was kind of bad planning on Mom's part, because Dad makes it a point to never work on the weekends, and going to the store on a Saturday counts as work. Even when you call to say it's on fire. My mom's intentions were good. She thought it would be the perfect location—a free venue with lots of tables and chairs already set up for people to sit and eat on.

Donovan finally got my dad to come over by telling him he forgot to re-up the store's insurance policy and the fire was spreading quickly. My dad arrived in under a minute. By that time, people had already started eating and my dad spent the rest of the party passing out coasters and trying to sell some of his inventory to his friends. "Feel that chair you're sitting on" and "See the detail on that table" doesn't put people in a very celebratory mood. You can see where my suspicions about parties come from.

There was another reason I wasn't looking forward to this baby shower. Veronica had warned me about what goes on at these things. Games. Lots of them. Like baby bingo, where you write down what gifts you think the mommy-to-be will get and as she opens them you cross them off on your game board. Veronica also told me about a game where the hostess puts baby items on a tray and you have to guess how much everything cost. Another game involves marking on a long piece of ribbon how big you think the mommy-to-be's stomach is, and then the ribbon is wrapped around her belly to find the winner. Yet another game is where you're given a roll of toilet paper and you have to diaper yourself. The last game Veronica told me about is where you are blindfolded and have to guess what kind of baby food you are eating. I wouldn't have brought this up except I glanced at Grace's baby shower agenda and saw each of those games on the schedule. That meant as soon as Amy showed up we were going to play them. And since I helped talk Amy into keeping her baby, I had to play these stupid games with a smile.

We put our gifts on top of the pile of presents and sat around in a circle staring at each other. This is a game I don't mind playing. Lauren and Madison were there, Alice of course and Shawna, some girl Jack's going out with. She kept giving the other girls the evil eye. Not sure what her problem was. Grace kept trying to call Adrian out from the bedroom. That girl must spend about ninety percent of her time in bed. If I did that my dad would immediately get suspicious and spend the whole day trying to find the guy hidden in there. Of course, he would never find him and I'd be banned from my bedroom except for set sleeping hours. Adrian needs a dad around who'll do that for her.

I was winning the staring in a circle game when one of Adrian's neighbors came in asking for Mom. We ran out to the stairway and found Amy sitting there eating chips and salsa. My first thought was, If she's going to skip out on her own shower she could have at least invited me. But it wasn't her fault; she wasn't able to walk because she was having labor pains. Lucky. Mom thought it was too early, but the look on Amy's face told me this was it. My own nephew got me out of a party I didn't want to be at even though it was his! I am loving this kid already.

I called Dad so he could meet us at the hospital. He thought I was kidding and wanted to know if I told Mom I was moving in with him. I told him I didn't have a chance, since it wasn't the right time, and now with Amy going into labor it REALLY wasn't the right time (at this point I say let's just move all my stuff to the new place and when Mom notices my room is empty she'll eventually figure it out). He finally got the message I wasn't kidding around and told me he was on his way. It might have gone quicker if I had told him I was on fire (with a crummy insurance policy).

6:12 P.M.

At the hospital, we all played the same sit around and stare at each other game we played at the shower. It's a lot more fun with hors d'oeuvres. Amy was getting restless and so was the baby. Mom told us to take a walk and get rid of some of the nervous energy, which is kind of tough to do in a hospital.

I was hoping Dad would tell Mom I was moving in with him while Amy and I walked around. Maybe the impending arrival of her first grandson will take the sting out of her younger daughter moving to another nest.

Amy told me Henry says hello. I can't believe that guy is still on the rebound. He really needs to get back with Alice. We're both strong women, but I think she probably likes the way he stares more than I do. That's when I'll know I've found the one for me—when I let him get away with the little things that normally bug me.

I hope he exists. He must. I mean, if Amy and Ben found each other . . .

It was at this moment I wished Amy knew more about Thomas. We aren't hanging out anymore and I wanted to talk about it. I think I might have offended him by suggesting he get another dog too soon. That or telling him his mom should skip the cupcake convention in Las Vegas and spend some time at home with him. But since Amy was about to give birth, I felt we should talk only about subjects relating to her. Not like we haven't been doing that for the last eight and a half months, but what can I say? Skipping the baby shower put me in a good mood.

While Amy and I walked around, I couldn't help thinking about how much has happened this year. Amy got pregnant, then got a boyfriend, my parents separated, my dad moved out and then moved back (garage adjacent), my mom got a new job and a boyfriend, and soon my dad and I are moving out. And now we're all here together to welcome this new baby into our lives. I just hope Mom sees that even though I won't be living with her anymore, we'll always be together. We'll never miss the important stuff.

I asked Amy if she was scared. I'm scared and I'm not even having the baby, so I knew her answer would be yes, but figured I'd ask anyway because sometimes when you're scared it helps to talk about it. She said she was but couldn't wait to meet her son. She wondered if I was going to help out with him. Of course I am—how could she ask me that? She asked if I was moving out so the baby would have a nursery. Wow, Amy has big plans for my room already. I had a feeling. The past couple of times she came into my room to "talk" her eyes seemed to wander around, distracted. Perhaps wondering where to put the crib and what color to paint the walls?

Then Amy asked me to be in the hospital room when she gave birth. If I had written this journal in pencil I would have gone back and erased the line: "I'll do anything Amy asks." I did mean it when I said I wanted to be there for Amy and the baby . . . and technically I was there . . . in the building. Emotionally I am so there. Hello, who fought for Amy to keep this kid? Me, his aunt, and this journal is documented proof of that. But I don't think his actual entrance is as important as, say, his entire life. But I could tell by the way Amy looked at me it was important to her. So I said yes. I would be in the room when she gave birth. But that doesn't mean I'm going to keep my eyes open.

Ben showed up and I let them have a moment alone. Who knows how many of those they'll get once the baby comes? Watching them together reminded me of the first time he called Amy and she had no idea who he was. Things have really changed.

I walked back to the waiting room and saw Mom and Dad talking. They weren't arguing, so I don't think Dad told Mom about my big move yet. They actually seemed to be enjoying each other's company. Dad was even giving Mom this intense, loving look, and something told me even though we were moving away from home, we would be back soon.

Feb. 5th

9:19 P.M.

Looks like my nephew likes to take his time . . . just like Amy in the mornings.

Since Amy doesn't like Dad and me joking around in everyday life, I don't know why we thought it would be a good idea to joke with her while she was in labor. Bad idea. Very bad idea.

But the good thing about labor is it stops Amy from getting too dramatic. Those contractions are quite effective at stopping her mid-sentence before she erupts like a volcano. They got so bad I had to get Mom.

I bet this whole situation will make parents rethink sending their kids to band camp. The once shining reputation of a summer spent with brassy instruments has been tainted by teen pregnancy. I should have a shirt made for Amy that says, "I went to band camp and all I got was this lousy baby."

Amy has never told me exactly what happened at band camp. I know she had sex with Ricky, but I've often wondered what led up to that fateful night. I bet Ricky sat on the benches during band rehearsal one day and thought, "Who haven't I slept with here?" Then he saw Amy and her fate was sealed. Amy never had a boyfriend before Ben . . . well, not a legitimate one anyway (hand-holding during lunch period in middle school doesn't count), and was probably so flattered by Ricky's attention she let her guard drop pretty easily . . . among other things.

I found Mom in the waiting room talking on the phone to Mimsy. Mimsy hasn't let Alzheimer's slow her down. She has a new boyfriend. Mom started to tell her about Thomas, but I told her we were already over. I was kind of relieved to finally talk about it with someone, even if that someone was Mom. I told her the details later. I met Thomas at our usual bus stop and broke it off. He asked if it was because I wanted to see other people. I told him I didn't want to see anybody at the moment. He wasn't too broken up about it. I heard he's already found another "bus stop" he likes better anyway. It happens. Our relationship wasn't exactly founded on honesty and the only thing we had in common were conspiracy theories and lying about our age. And once that gets old . . . well, the truth is usually kind of boring.

I should take up ballet again. I took a few classes over the summer in secret because I missed it so much, but Dad caught me dancing, so it didn't feel like mine anymore. I also ran into Lauren at the ballet studio, because she takes classes there as well. And the fact that we had something in common really scared me. And of course she blabbed about it to Amy. Amy didn't care because, unbeknownst to me at the time, she had other things on her mind.

I used to dance a lot when I was little but dropped out because black tutus weren't allowed. Mom was surprised I liked ballet. She expected me to like interpretive performance art, but interpretive performance art is such a waste of time. I'd rather just say what I'm thinking instead of wrapping myself in tin foil and spinning around, waiting for everyone to figure it out on their own.

Ballet takes concentration and strength. The concentration part is especially tough when your ballet class is located between the cha cha dance studio and the belly-dancing classes. And when Lauren keeps trying to talk to you and you don't want to talk to her. I wanted to give it my full attention because I thought it would help me. The truth is I'm nervous about starting high school soon. I know it's still about a year away and I said I can handle anything, but the anticipation of something is always the worst. Ballet was always comforting because I could focus my nervous energy into it. But I thought if people knew I was taking ballet they'd see it as a sign of weakness.

That's why I'm grateful Dad didn't tell Mom I took up ballet again. I've got a dark reputation to uphold, after all. I stopped practicing ballet once school started and Amy's pregnancy was revealed, but it's an escape I kind of need right now. And it allows me to think instead of blurting out the kind of things that make Mom so angry.

I told Mom Amy needed her and took her seat in the waiting room. I'm not in a hurry to get back in there until it's definitely time . . . and even then I won't be in too much of a hurry. I wish Amy would change her mind about wanting me in there for the birth. I know everything that's supposed to happen and would therefore rather not see it.

Ricky showed up and sat with me. I don't think he really had a choice. He wasn't ready to go in there yet and face everybody. I don't blame him. My family is a tough crowd. And I'd know—I'm the toughest one. And Amy isn't exactly in a very happy, talky mood. I'm not sure why he thought I'd be any better. It's probably because we haven't spoken that much in the time we've known each other. He'll learn.

He said he felt bad Amy was going through all this right now. He didn't seem too concerned about her when he had sex with her eight and a half months ago. He promised he'd be a father to the baby, and I said if he broke his promise I would pretty much kill him. He didn't appreciate my threats, but there's a lot about him I don't appreciate. Since he's still getting to know me he continued our conversation. He asked what Amy was naming the baby. I said I didn't know but it's not going to be Ricky Junior (at least it better not be!).

He asked if I was this mean to Ben. I almost felt bad for him. He's always going to be compared to Ben from now on, since Ben's closer to Amy than Ricky can ever be, even though Amy's having Ricky's baby. But he has to deal with it. And he needs a tougher skin. I can help him with that.

I told him I'm not mean to Ben because Ben's not the one who put Amy in this situation. I know Amy needs to take some responsibility, but Ricky also needs to stop playing the victim. By telling him the truth, I am being a friend to him. Not the kind of friend he wants, but the one he needs. I asked him if he's even capable of being a friend. He didn't answer, which worried me. I mean, it wasn't a trick question.

So I decided to set him straight because now was the perfect time. I told him the only way I would be his friend is if he takes care of Amy and is there for his son.

He looked at me like he was going to play the victim again, but he didn't. He nodded and said I was right. He was looking at the situation all wrong. Instead of looking at how it is, he needs to look at how it's going to be. He can be a friend to Amy. And he and Ben can be friends. And they can all be in his son's life. Then he smiled and said he and I could be friends, too.

I didn't smile back. I told him I'll believe it when I see it.

I guess we'll see.

Feb. 6th

1:30 P.M.

HAPPY BIRTHDAY, BABY!!! (And good luck, you'll need it.)

It was beginning to seem like this kid was as scared of the birth as Amy. I'm surprised they didn't tell us to go home and come back tomorrow. Amy's gotten the most sleep of her life here, which is good, since she's about to live without it very soon. I wanted her to wake up and start pushing so we could meet her son and go home. The hospital's an okay place for a few hours, but soon you begin to feel like you should go ahead and check into a room.

Ben walked in with his video camera, so we could use it to film the birth of the baby. I can say, with the utmost confidence, that that baby will never watch himself being born. I know my nephew. Ben agreed it did sound ridiculous, but Amy wanted it filmed. And she wanted me to film it.

She wanted me to zoom in and out, get close-ups and wide shots, coverage . . . so nothing about the birth would be missed. Someone needs to lower the dose on her pain meds so she's able to think clearly, because this is nuts. I planned on standing there with my eyes closed and now she wants a birth documentary?

Then Ben started with the "I love you's" to Amy. Combined with her diary poetry, they're a match made in cheesy heaven.

Dad and I waited outside until it was time. He was glad to know that every minute we're in this hospital I'm another year away from having sex. Dad says maybe I should live in the hospital instead of with him. I don't even want to think how many years will be added on when I film the birth . . . we're talking a decade, at least.

NO CLUE ABOUT THE DATE OR TIME—IT PRETTY MUCH STOOD STILL! A.M./P.M. WHATEVER!!!

I DID IT. IT'S OVER. THE BABY'S HERE. I THINK I GOT EVERYTHING ON FILM. I TRIED, AT LEAST. WHILE I WAS IN THERE I THOUGHT OF A BUSINESS AMY AND I COULD START. WE COULD MASS-PRODUCE THIS VIDEO I JUST

SHOT AND SHOW IT IN EVERY SCHOOL IN AMERICA. THIS
VIDEO WILL BE ONE HUNDRED PERCENT EFFECTIVE IN
PROMOTING ABSTINENCE. WE WOULD MAKE MILLIONS
OF DOLLARS AND NEVER HAVE TO WORK AGAIN, AMY'S
BABY WOULD BE SET FOR LIFE, HIS COLLEGE EDUCATION
WOULD BE PAID FOR, AND HE COULD RETIRE YOUNG.

SINCE MY DAD WILL NEVER SEE THIS JOURNAL, I FEEL
OKAY IN SAYING HE WAS RIGHT. I'M NEVER HAVING SEX
IN MY WHOLE, WHOLE LIFE. IF I EVER WANT A KID I WILL
ADOPT AND LOVE THE CHILD LIKE HE/SHE IS MY OWN,
BECAUSE THAT LOOKED LIKE THE MOST PAINFUL, UN-
NATURAL THING IN THE WORLD. I CAN'T BELIEVE SOME
PEOPLE HAVE MORE THAN ONE CHILD. I CAN APPRECI-
ATE THE MIRACLE OF LIFE IN A NEW WAY AND THAT NEW
WAY IS TRYING TO FORGET ABOUT WHAT I JUST SAW FOR
THE REST OF MY LIFE. THERE. I'M DONE. I'M NEVER TALK-
ING ABOUT THIS AGAIN.

Sorry about that. I'm calmer now. Well, not calmer, but a
little less hysterical. The birth was everything I thought it'd
be, which wasn't exactly a good thing. There was a lot of
screaming and complaining and medical things going on. I
guess the word I'm looking for is "gross." It was very gross.
And it's on camera, but I don't know who's going to watch it.
I'm certainly not going to recommend it to anyone outside of
my previously mentioned business plan.

Dad had a huge smile on his face when I came out into the
hallway. He said I looked like I wasn't thinking about sex.
He's got that right.

After everything had calmed down, Amy had visitors come in and see the baby. I have to admit my nephew is the cutest baby I've ever seen. I'm glad I worked so hard to keep him. I can tell we're going to be close and he's going to fit in perfectly with the family. He came out screaming, so he definitely knows how to pick a fight. The next test will be how he handles living in a house with all of us. I mean a house with Mom and Amy, with frequent visits from me and Dad.

When I was looking at him, I started having second thoughts about living with Dad. Did I really want to be out of the house? I might miss a lot of firsts. Walking, teething, talking. I really want to be there when he starts talking. I have lots of words and phrases to teach him, like "no," "prove it," and "we'll see about that."

But the more I thought about it the more I realized not being in the house doesn't mean I won't be in his life. A home is where you make it and it doesn't have to be in just one place. The baby's a part of my home, even if he's not down the hall. Also, if he were down the hall, I'd be losing sleep because of the screaming. He's cute now but the screaming monster (that's Veronica's term) will come out soon. Yeah, I can live without the screaming in the middle of the night.

Feb. 7th

When Mom, Dad, and I came home, we were all exhausted. But Dad thought it would be best if we moved to the new place right away. Better to get settled than put it off. Like ripping off a Band-Aid. I gave Mom a hug and she walked Dad and me outside to the moving truck. Some of our neighbors were even outside to see us off. They looked grateful that the George Juergens boxer shorts fashion show was moving to a different venue.

Mom got very emotional, probably because she'd just witnessed a birth and now she was watching a departure. I knew she would be, but I was surprised by how sad she got. She said how much she was going to miss me and miss seeing me around. She's been so preoccupied with Amy I forgot how much she cared. She told me I can come home anytime. That was the plan all along. Did she think I wasn't ever going to come back? Dad told me to tell her I love her, which I did. I was just enjoying the attention so much I forgot Mom needed some from me, too. I said, "I love you," and we pulled the truck out and parked it next door.

Dad had filled me in on the fact that we were moving next door during one of our many hours at the hospital. I didn't know if I was happy about it at first, but then Dad gave his "together yet apart" speech and told me if all marriages consisted of two houses then the divorce rate would go down dramatically.

I expected Mom to get angry and glare at my dad because he essentially moved only ten feet from the garage. But she got even MORE EMOTIONAL (so did the neighbors, but they were on the other end of the spectrum). Happy even. She seemed relieved that something actually worked out right for once. Of course, she might change her mind after Dad starts dropping by regularly.

11:02 A.M.

We went back to the hospital to check on Amy and the baby. I was kind of sick of saying "the baby this" and "the baby that."

He won't be a baby for very long, he needs a name, I told her. So that's the first thing I asked Amy. I thought she'd have a name picked out by now but she didn't. Amy said I should name him, since I convinced her to keep him. I thought about something simple that would go with Juergens. Because we Juergenses are a complicated package, and he needs a solid name he can count on. I suggested John. Amy really liked it. John Juergens. JJ. See, it even works as a cool nickname. It's my job as John's aunt to think of these things.

I tried to get out of going to school today, but Dad wouldn't budge. No one should see what I have seen and then have to go to school right away. He told me he's seen more than me, and he's still going to work. I thought living with him would have its perks, but they're not kicking in yet.

We were going to see John before he dropped me off at school, but Mom's new boyfriend, David the architect, was there. I guess I can't drop by whenever I feel like it, because I don't feel like being around her boyfriend. I don't know why I thought all the other problems would go away now that Amy had had the baby and I had moved in with Dad. When Dad showed me the house, it seemed perfect. A new house, a new beginning, and new possibilities. But what I didn't realize until after our first night there was we didn't move away from our problems, we moved next door to them.

Seeing Mom's new boyfriend make himself at home next door kicked in Dad's midlife crisis a little early. He's going to buy a motorcycle. He said I could get a puppy. I don't mind if he has a crisis if it means I get a puppy. I do mind Mom's boyfriend bringing over big stuffed animals for my nephew, though.

I don't know what made me think of this, but it just suddenly popped into my head. It was this trip we took with Mimsy up north. It was our first trip with just us and without Mom and Dad. Mom had questioned Mimsy about everything a million times before we left. She didn't really trust Mimsy to have everything covered. We had planned to stay at this great hotel the first night, but we never made it there. The car broke down and then Amy got carsick even though we weren't technically in the car. Then we lost the hotel reservations and had to stay at this other hotel that wasn't up to code. It was almost like camping, except we had an actual toilet but it didn't flush. I looked it up online and believe it or not, it's still there. I can't believe that place is still standing.

Mimsy had to call Mom from a pay phone because the hotel didn't have phones in the room. Mom asked Mimsy how everything was going and Mimsy would only say, "Fine," and we were ahead of schedule. When Mom questioned us about the trip, I went literal again. "Fun," "fine," and "great" were my answers to all of her questions. Mom still doesn't know what really happened.

It seemed like we were never going to make it home. But we did. And you know what?

It was the best trip I've ever taken in my life. That's why I think things are going to be okay. I didn't plan for Amy to get pregnant or for Mom and Dad to get divorced, but because of these things Amy and I have gotten really close. I guess what I'm trying to say is, I'm grateful for everything that's happened these last nine months, both good and bad. And I just realized who this journal is really for. Principal Miller, if it's possible, could you return my journal after you finish reading it? There's someone I would like to give it to. When he's old enough, that is. . . .

John, I hope you enjoyed reading your aunt Ashley's journal. It's weird to think of you as a teenager reading something I wrote when I was your age. I hope I'm still the same way now as I was when I wrote this. You'll have to tell me.

So that's it from me. I've completed my assignment. I've journaled my emotions to death and hope maybe I'll be understood a little better.

At least until I get to high school.

Aug. 23rd

I'm back.

I know what you're thinking. My belly button got me into trouble again and I'm being forced to continue writing in this journal as my creative outlet. Wrong. Believe it or not, I want to write in this journal. Not for Principal Miller, but for myself. After I finished my prison sentence here (so long, Principal Miller!) and had my summer vacation, so many things happened. I ended up writing stuff down on little scraps of paper and hiding them around my room until I could get my journal back. Which I finally did thanks to Kurt, the locker tagger, who stood guard while I broke into Principal Miller's office using bobby pins. I found my journal in the bottom of her closet. Who called that one? If you forgot, please refer to the beginning of this journal.

This is why I needed the same journal, so I could refer back to things.

Since Amy brought John back from the hospital things have been kind of crazy. I told Amy I would help take care of my nephew so she wouldn't give him up for adoption, but she quickly took advantage of this privilege. One night, Amy wanted me to watch John so she could sleep. And sleep. And sleep. She slept for the whole day. Mom, Dad, and I each tried to wake her up, but she would only mumble, "Just five more minutes," then turn over. It got to the point where I was taking care of John more than Amy was. My dad even said to me one day, "Who had this baby, you or Amy?" Thanks to Veronica's training I was good at taking care of my nephew. I'm kind of maternal when I want to be.

So Operation Take Care of John Yourself was put into action. I had to give Amy some tough love because that was the only way she was going to adapt to her new situation. I stopped answering my cell phone and pretended I wasn't home when she knocked on the door, asking for help. Dad and I became very good floor crawlers.

And Amy became good at taking care of John. Except for one time when I watched her try to microwave leftovers in the refrigerator and she stared at the icemaker for one minute and twenty-two seconds before realizing what she'd done, but other than that she's getting the hang of it.

I was hoping this past summer would be boring for every-one, and it started out that way. Amy had to go to summer school because of all the school she missed when John was born. She was pretty upset about it. She wanted to take John to Italy so she could be with Ben, who was working at his un-cle's hotel, over the summer. Like Mom and Dad would have ever allowed that to happen.

I was relieved Amy couldn't go to Italy. In my opinion, she and Ben needed a break. Ben was getting very jealous of Ricky and his relationship with Amy and John, and Amy was too exhausted to give Ben the amount of attention he needed.

Ricky, it turns out, is a natural father. He kept his promise to me in the hospital. He was being a friend to Amy and tak-ing care of John. He is the only one who is able to get John to stop crying just by picking him up. You'd think Amy would be thrilled but it's the opposite. It makes her angry because she's the one who takes care of him the most, but he won't stop crying for her. Sometimes I listen outside Amy's room when Ricky is putting John down for the night. Ricky likes to tell John a story before he leaves. It could be something that happened to him that day, or a nice memory he has from one of his foster families. One night he told John about watch-ing Amy run into people while practicing marching at band camp. Hearing stories like these, I wonder if Ricky and Amy will ever end up together, if Amy ever looks at Ricky and feels a twinge of those same feelings she had for him at band camp. I have to admit, Ricky taking responsibility for his son is attractive, and Amy must feel the same way when she's tired and Ricky's there to help.

One night I forgot to return the baby monitor to Amy and happened to overhear her and Ricky talking. Ricky was telling Amy he thinks John has made him into a better person, and he thought Amy had played a part in that as well. Then he thanked her for being the mother of his child. Then it was quiet for a bit, like they were hugging or something. Amy asked Ricky if he thought they would have ever been friends if it weren't for John. Ricky said he didn't want to think about a world without John. Or her.

Ben has a reason to be jealous.

Dad wasn't worried about Ricky. Dad, of course, was only worried Amy and Ben were having sex. I told him Ben and Amy weren't having sex. He wasn't convinced I really knew because we don't live with Mom and Amy anymore and how could I be so sure? Most of the time Amy is too tired to even shower, let alone give Ben any alone time. Babies really are the best birth control. That seemed to give him peace of mind.

Dad didn't seem to be as worried about Mom, but I was. The stress from John seemed to be getting to her. At first I thought she was just gaining weight, but soon it was all too familiar. Her hands and feet were swollen and she was tired all the time. The same signs Amy showed last summer. Mimsy agreed with my suspicions about Mom being pregnant. Sure, she has Alzheimer's and thinks Mom is pregnant with me, but she also recognized the pregnancy patterns.

Who is less than half her age! Part of me wants to give her a high five and the other part wants to cover my ears.

Dad should really be worried that Mimsy has no problem answering any sex questions I have, no matter how inappropriate. So I asked how sex was with her new, younger boyfriend.

She said it's great and she's finally at her sexual peak, so she needs a younger man to keep up with her.

Mom did eventually admit she was pregnant. Dad was shocked, and then relieved when she said it wasn't his. I wish it was Dad's because I don't like David. At all. And he doesn't like me either. I overheard him tell Mom I made him nervous. I find it very odd to be in the same situation as last year where someone in this family is pregnant and the father is somewhat of a mystery. I know Mom said the baby's not his and Dad said he had a vasectomy ten years ago, so the baby can't be his. If that's true, why was he even nervous in the first place?

Mom and I were at the market one day and I was trying to get up the nerve to ask if it's really Dad's baby, but I got sidetracked when NedTed started following me around the store. That's when Grace tapped me on the shoulder. I will always be grateful to her for that.

Her dad had recently passed away and I told her how sorry I was and that I wasn't going to make her talk about it. I'm sure she was tired of talking about it anyway. She seemed to appreciate my honesty. She asked if I remembered our conversation at Amy and Ben's wedding reception, about us being like sisters even though we aren't related by blood. I told her I remembered. She said since her dad died she made a promise to herself not to take her family for granted

I didn't write to her, not because I didn't want to but because I was following up on some things. More on that later.

and wanted to include me in that promise. I told her I appreciated that, but with my newborn nephew and sibling on the way, I was getting more family than I could handle. She said she understood but was wondering if she could e-mail me while she went to her premed summer program. I said what is that, like medical camp? She said yeah, she's thinking of following in her dad's footsteps. She told me I didn't have to write her back, she just wanted to keep in touch over the summer. I told her she could write to me, but I probably wouldn't write her back.

Grace kept her word. She wrote me every day over the summer. Every. Day. She talked about her daily routine at camp: In the mornings she would listen to one of the camp physicians lecture for about an hour. Then she would follow another camp physician on his hospital rounds to observe how he interacted with his patients. At lunch she and the rest of her group would talk with their camp physician about the different patient cases they saw that morning. After lunch, she would sit in on her camp physician's office hours and see any patients that came in. At the end of the day, she would write about her various experiences with the patients and how she would have handled it the same or differently from her mentoring physician.

The e-mails were pretty boring at first (we all know how I feel about camp and science), until she mentioned that Lauren's brother, Jason, was attending the same medical camp and they were in the same lecture group and did their hospital rounds together. They quickly became good friends. One day they were picked to demonstrate the proper techniques involved in CPR. Grace was the victim and Jason performed CPR on her. But eventually he forgot all about chest compressions and decided to concentrate solely on the mouth-to-mouth part. Grace said after that day anything they did together became fraught with sexual tension. It finally culminated when Grace had to give Jason a basic physical. She checked all his vital signs, including listening to his heart with her stethoscope. His heart was pounding so fast Grace thought he might have high blood pressure. Then they kissed. Funny that Grace never mentioned Jack once in any of her e-mails. Eventually, Grace and Jason decided to be friends. Well, Grace acts as if they came to this decision because they are two mature adults, but I think what caused her second thoughts was the patient with the raging case of syphilis she mentioned treating in her previous e-mail.

I love having information before Lauren and Madison. I intend to keep it to myself and enjoy the moment when they find out on their own. Unlike them, I don't intend to blab things all over town. I wonder if Madison would be upset to know Jason was cheating on her with Grace. It seems like it would be hard to be mad at Grace, though. She seems like a genuinely good person.

Amy and Ben weren't talking over the summer because when Ben came to say good-bye the morning of his flight to Bologna, Ricky was there and it looked like he had spent the night in Amy's room. No matter how many times Amy called Ben, he never picked up. She really has no imagination. I got through right away, but not on Ben's cell phone.

This was the lead I was talking about. I bought a prepaid telephone card and called the front desk of Ben's uncle's hotel. Some guy named Gio answered. He was the concierge for the hotel so he liked to talk to people and knew many languages, including English. I asked if Ben was taking advantage of everything Bologna had to offer and I was not referring to sightseeing. Gio didn't understand what I meant and said Ben was doing a lot of sightseeing. He ascended the Torre degli Asinelli, visited the Basilica di San Petronio, walked the 666 arches to the hilltop Santuario della Madonna di San Luca, and has had enough pasta bolognese to last him a lifetime. He has also been well versed in prosciutto, mortadella, and salame, which should help when he returns to work at the butcher shop.

I asked if there was anything or anyone else he's been seeing in Bologna. Gio paused, then said, "You mean, besides the girl?" Gio went on to tell me Ben has been spending all his free time with the daughter of a family friend. When he ascended the Torre degli Asinelli, she raced him to the top. When Ben was admiring the Basilica di San Petronio, she pointed out its unfinished façade. She was there coaching Ben up all 666 arches until they arrived together at the hilltop

Santuario della Madonna di San Luca. And during breaks from all this sightseeing, she has taken him to all her favorite restaurants. I asked if she's ever spent the night. Gio said sure, but all they do is talk. He hears them whenever he walks by. That Ben sure is a talker. So I asked if he's ever mentioned Amy. Gio asked, "Who?" I said Amy, his girlfriend in America. Then he said, "I have not heard of this Amy that you speak of." He asked if I was Amy. I said no and hung up.

I didn't want to tell Amy what Gio told me because it was probably nothing, even if it could be something. And I didn't want her bad mood ruining my summer. She had Ricky around, so what if she didn't have Ben? She still had the rest of the summer to get used to that, which was probably a good thing if Ben comes back and breaks up with her.

A couple of really bad things happened recently. David proposed to Mom, and Dad was served with divorce papers. That's one of the unfortunate parts of living next door to your ex. You're able to hide in the bushes and see your ex-wife get proposed to by her new boyfriend. Plus, your mom notices when you've skipped school.

Mom hasn't accepted David's proposal, but the divorce papers aren't a good sign. David also wants Mom to move to a house near Mimsy. I don't like the possibility of people leaving again. Amy's going to need someone around to help her, and with Mom gone that would mean Dad and me sharing diaper duty.

Pretty soon it was time for high school orientation. As I was getting out of the car, my dad said, "Don't drink, don't do drugs, and don't get pregnant." I asked him if there was anything else. He said, "Yeah, make some friends, will ya?" I'm not so sure about the friends part and as for getting pregnant, if I do ever decide to have a baby I'm hoping science has advanced enough where I can grow my baby in some kind of hospital incubator and pick it up nine months later. I know I've said I don't trust science, but if that were to become a reality it would make up for all the times science has failed me in the past.

It took only two minutes for me to walk into the wrong classroom. And I know it was the wrong one because I found Jack and Madison making out. They didn't even notice me until I asked if this was sex ed. Jack stuttered that it was a meeting of the Dead Parents Club and asked if I had a dead parent. Madison slapped him on the arm and said I didn't. They asked me to please forget what I saw, since Madison is dating Jason and Jack is dating Grace. I wanted so badly to tell them their significant others weren't wasting any time either, but instead I asked if they got over their grief by making out. Madison shrugged and said one day they just admitted they found the other person attractive and decided to see how it felt to . . . kiss. And kiss some more. But it's just a summer thing; it doesn't mean they don't care about Grace and Jason. It's just an experiment. Like science. I said more like cheating, but whatever makes them feel less guilty. Jack asked if I was going to tell anyone I saw him and Madison kissing. I said no, but they might want to lock the door next time.

So orientation was pretty lame. I had to take a standardized English and math test and then write a dreaded essay describing who I am in 300 words or less. I was offended by the assumption it would take only 300 words to describe Ashley Juergens, so I spent 287 explaining why I thought the question was both trite and offensive. Ironically, I think that will give them a better idea of who I am than if I had actually answered the stupid question.

After testing we went to the auditorium for a Grant High School pep rally, where various students from the different clubs and sports groups gave presentations on why their extracurricular activity was most worth our spare time. Then the cheerleaders did a cheer about what it takes to be a great student: "What will make you cool? Doing your homework right after school! Don't rest until you've studied for that test!" And my personal favorite, "High school is grand when you join a club, play a sport, or march in band!" Maybe I should start my own club, Ironics Anonymous.

At lunch I sat alone. I know Dad wanted me to make friends, but I have so much on my mind I wanted to be alone with my thoughts. I wondered if maybe I have too much baggage to have friends. Who would want to listen to me talk about Amy, John, and my dysfunctional parents all the time? Sure, it's interesting at first, but after a while it gets exhausting. At one point someone asked if the seat next to me was taken. I said it wasn't and she dragged the chair to a nearby table that didn't have any more empty seats. That's when I started thinking maybe I should consider making some friends in high school.

I ran into Amy as she was leaving her history summer school class. She was checking her phone for any messages from Ben but there weren't any. I checked my phone and read a text message Gio the concierge had sent me: *Ben and "special" friend update: They shared gelato and watched the sunset together.* I didn't tell Amy what I knew. I figured what she didn't know couldn't hurt her. And maybe there isn't anything to know. Ben and this mystery girl are probably just friends. At least I'm hoping. It would make my life simpler. It would be nice to go in that direction for once.

Mom said the baby's been kicking a lot. That settles it. That baby is one hundred percent Juergens. It's feisty and it likes to show it. If it were David's, Mom would be having the most boring pregnancy ever. Screw science, I'm going off general observation on this one. We'll see if I'm wrong. I've rarely been so far!

It's going to be strange to have a little brother or sister who's fourteen years younger. Even stranger than having a nephew who is older than said brother or sister. I know I can handle it, but my younger sibling's going to put a big dent in my high school social life. What if I get a boyfriend and he sees that Amy has a baby and Mom has a baby? He'll think I have the most fertile genes on the planet and run off. My dad would love that.

It's a weird thing to get used to at this stage in my life. Two babies and two houses. It might soon be one house. Adrian came over to ask my dad if he was interested in selling the house to her family. At first I was worried she was here to take my bed or hug my dad. She probably wants the house so she can spy on Ricky. I don't care so much about that, but I'm not sure how I feel about Dad's ex-girlfriend moving in next door. And I don't know if Mom would welcome us back home. Especially since she might be engaged and Dad might be the father of her baby.

I'm not looking forward to next summer. What's next, someone has twins? Triplets? I'm not going to get pregnant, so something else will have to happen to get Lauren and Madison gossiping.

I'm about to start high school and see Amy and her friends all day, every day. I might even make a friend or two of my own, maybe even start dating. . . . Which means I'm going to have even more to write about.

I guess I'll have to buy a new journal.

Relive The Drama On DVD

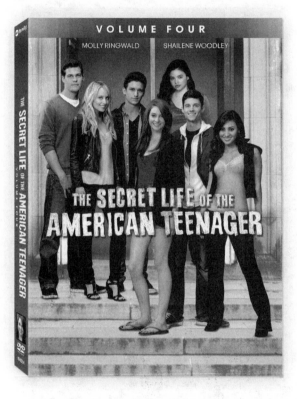

Collect Them All Today!

ALL NEW
MONDAYS

THE SECRET LIFE
OF THE
AMERICAN TEENAGER

all new episodes
mondays at 8/7c

©ABC Family